The Only Way Home

R. M. Kaye

PublishAmerica
Baltimore

© 2008 by R. M. Kaye.
All rights reserved. No part of this book may be reproduced, stored in a retrieval system or transmitted in any form or by any means without the prior written permission of the publishers, except by a reviewer who may quote brief passages in a review to be printed in a newspaper, magazine or journal.

First printing

All characters in this book are fictitious, and any resemblance to real persons, living or dead, is coincidental.

PublishAmerica has allowed this work to remain exactly as the author intended, verbatim, without editorial input.

ISBN: 1-10672-396-0
PUBLISHED BY PUBLISHAMERICA, LLLP
www.publishamerica.com
Baltimore

Printed in the United States of America

The Only Way Home

Dearest Heather,

Always remember the brightest light to guide you on your path comes from within.

God Bless,
R. M. Kaye

This book is dedicated to my sister Marie, without her it would not have been possible. You are an inspiration and a guiding light to anyone who is fortunate enough to know you.

~1~

*'Come to me, all you who are weary and burdened
and I will give you rest.'*
Matthew 11:28 (NIV)

He sat on the steps of the school wondering how long it would take for Justin to get out of detention for coming late to class one too many times. The sky rumbled as dark rain clouds moved into his view. 'What a perfect ending to a perfectly horrible day,' he thought to himself. Aaron had forgotten his lunch money, gotten into an argument with his best friend Mack, and just found out that as of the last test he was getting a D in History. At least his mom and step dad were planning on a dinner out tonight. He was looking forward to being home alone and getting on his computer with no one reminding him of how long he has been rotting his brain.

Aaron felt the first drips of rain on his head when Gus, Paul, and Teddy walked through the front doors of the school. Aaron was not in the mood for the three bullies. He wondered what they would do when there wasn't a teacher within shouting distance. Aaron has had to put up with Gus and his cohorts for nearly two years and each time they had an encounter it seemed to be getting worse.

It started out with name calling, but has since progressed to pushing and tripping in the school hallways. Last week Gus sucker punched him in the back as he was on his way to third hour, which was the last straw for Aaron. Gus was bigger than Aaron by a good thirty pounds but Aaron didn't care. He threw himself at the larger boy and they went to the ground both trying to inflict as much pain as possible. The fight was broken up within a few minutes by a teacher and they each walked away with a few scratches and a stern warning from the principal.

He tried to pretend he didn't notice them and hoped they would just walk on by and leave him alone, he wasn't that lucky.

"Hey you guys, Speedy Gonzales is still hanging around," Paul laughed out.

"Looks like it's his lucky day, eh? No teachers to save you this time punk," Gus sneered, followed by grunts from the other two. Gus was known around school as a "druggie" and was feared by most of the boys that attended the high school.

Aaron could feel the heat of their stares on the back of his head. He stood up and turned to face his three tormentors hoping their arrival meant that detention was over and Justin would be out at any moment.

"I dare ya to teach him a lesson," Paul chuckled as he looked Aaron up and down with disgust. Paul ran his fingers through his shoulder length bleach blonde hair as his mocking grin revealed the braces on his teeth.

"Oh, he'll get a lesson alright," Gus scoffed, as he took a threatening step forward. "Come on Taco Bell, you ready for round two?"

"Don't you guys have anything better to do?" he tried to reason. When there was only some menacing chuckles in response he thought his chances for talking his way out of this were slim to none. "Gus, didn't I see you crying in the doctor's office last weekend? I was in the waiting room when you were leaving and I saw him give you a lollypop to make it better!" Aaron had been waiting for almost a week for Gus to try something so that he could use that little tidbit of information. He mistakenly thought that might put him into place but instead it made Gus's face turn three shades of red.

"You were crying at the doctor, Gus?!?" Teddy laughed so hard he doubled over and looked like he was close to peeing himself.

"What? Did you get a shot you big freaking baby?" choked out Paul. Now the two boys were leaning against the building holding onto one another for support because they were in such a fit of hysterics.

"If you guys don't shut up, I'm going to pound one of *you* into the ground," Gus bit out. Paul and Teddy immediately tried to recover but were both still biting on their lower lip trying to contain their laughter. "That's it chalupa you won't be thinking anything's funny when I get done with you."

Aaron tried to keep his temper in check but with each innuendo Gus threw at him his temper flared. Aaron tried to contain his growing fury by clenching and unclenching his fists. He took a step forward imagining he was ripping Gus to pieces. Gus ran at him like a steaming locomotive as Aaron braced himself for the impact that was sure to send him to the ground.

Both boys landed with a thud at the bottom of the stairs with the wind knocked out of them. Gus grabbed at Aarons hair as he tried to get out from beneath him and get his breath back. His whole body was quivering with a mixture of adrenaline and rage. He wasn't sure how, but he managed to get on top of Gus and started to pummel at the boys face. He was so furious he never noticed that the rain was now coming down in sheets. He was soaked through; he didn't know if it was the cold or the fury that had him shaking. Just then he felt a sharp pain on the back of his head and everything went black.

When Aaron regained consciousness he was laying on his side being kicked in his legs and stomach by Gus and Teddy while Paul was dumping the contents of his backpack to the ground. As Gus was about to kick him in the stomach again Aaron grabbed his leg and pushed up with all his might and sent the boy flying backwards into Paul who promptly followed suit. Aaron scrambled to his feet and despite the excruciating pain in his side and thigh, ran as fast as he could.

Rain was pelting down almost sideways through the streets making them empty of pedestrians. Aaron McKay ran through the narrow alleys of the small town in Michigan, out of breath and mindless of the harsh wind and rain, dodging dumpsters as if his very life depended on escape. He rounded the corner and searched desperately for a hiding place, his face white with terror. He noticed ornately carved, wooden double doors across the two lane street just as he heard the familiar taunting and laughing of his tormentors from the alley he just came from. The drenched dark haired boy ran blindly toward the safety they offered, praying silently they wouldn't be locked.

The screeching of tires and a car's horn tore him from his shocked state as a red Pontiac flew by, missing him by inches. The driver yelled out a few obscenities as he continued down Amber Street. Aaron wasted no more time reaching the refuge he so desperately needed. He never slowed down as he reached the large doors and hit them with such force they flew open wide and then slowly start to close again. He stumbled into a huge deserted entry way trying clumsily to get his balance so that he wouldn't fall.

Aaron scanned the room for a place to hide and noticed a large table along the right wall with a white table cloth that swayed gently to the floor. He decided that was as good a place as any and darted under it without another thought. He sat there shivering, hoping they wouldn't find him there. He couldn't take on all three boys no matter how mad he was.

THE ONLY WAY HOME

He choked back tears not from pain but from the insults that hurt far worse than any bruise ever could. "How can I stick up for myself when I don't even know why I look this way?" He whispered to himself. "My mom has blue eyes and blonde hair, so does most of my family, if I could only find my dad all of this would go away. Dad, why aren't you with me?" He could barely get the words out.

~2~

'The Lord is good, a refuge in times of trouble. He cares for those who trust in Him.' Nahum 1:7(NIV)

The boy curled into a ball and began sobbing, his rain soaked sweater and Nike's lying next to him on the floor. He didn't remember falling asleep but he awoke to the most beautiful sound he had ever heard. He had no idea how much time had passed but all he really cared about was finding the source of the sound.

Aaron cautiously peeked from under the table cloth making sure no one was there, and then left his hiding place. As he looked around he noticed the high vaulted ceilings and a huge sign above the table he was hiding under marked 'VISITORS CENTER' in bright blue letters. There was another table like the one he was under further up the entry way and on the opposite wall with a sign above it marked 'INFORMATION CENTER' next to a set of huge wooden double doors. And on either side of the table he had been hiding under there were hallways. The sound seemed to be coming from the large double doors to his left and his curiosity got the better of him.

He slowly made his way to the double doors and opened them as quietly as he could and peered inside. He saw rows and rows of maroon chairs in a room big enough to fit at least 800 people. There were spiral staircases on either side of the room leading up to a balcony with additional seating. To his right was a sort of stage with a podium and more chairs on its right and left side. Then he saw the source of the sound.

A choir of at least twenty-five was singing as a band played. "I'm in a church," he said to himself. He excused his ignorance in figuring out where he was because he had really only been in a church twice that he could remember. The first time was for his cousin's baptism and the second time was for a wedding. Aaron picked an inconspicuous spot next to the closest spiral staircase and settled down to listen.

The harmonious way the music mixed with the voices of the choir was unbelievable. Aaron closed his eyes and let the sounds flow through him.
"I am redeemed by You, delivered by You, freed by You; even though I don't deserve it You loved me anyway. When my days are long, and the weight of my dreams are heavy, You are my refuge, because You loved me anyway. Why have You ever cared? Why have I ever mattered to You? I will never know why You have loved me anyway. You are my Father and the only thing I need and all because You loved me anyway…" and the choir sang on.

Aaron stared intently at the choir with tears streaming down his face. He only wished that those words were true. He wanted there to be a place where he could be safe, safe from the torture of his mind, always wondering why his dad left him, why he wasn't there for him now, what did he do that made him not good enough. That there could be something out there to take away his pain, and give him the perfect place to hide from everyone including himself was too much to ever hope for.

"Why couldn't you have loved me anyway?" the softly whispered question revealed more to Aaron than he could ever realize. That was what he so desperately needed to know, and the only person who could answer that was his father. He realized at that moment he had to get that question answered no matter what the cost.

Aaron was shaken from his reverie by the buzzing of his pager. When he checked the number he was surprised to see Mack's number.

"I guess we're on speaking terms again," he thought out loud. He had to get home anyway. As he was walking out of the sanctuary he wondered what he was going to do about his backpack, at least there wasn't anything in there that was important.

When he arrived at the double doors he was startled by someone opening the doors from the other side as he was reaching for them. He took a quick step back and waited to see who was on the other side. A boy maybe two or three years older than him, with big brown eyes and sandy blonde hair appeared and smiled at him. Aaron could only smile back. He had never met a complete stranger before and felt so at ease just from a smile, it was bizarre.

"Hi there, I don't think I have met you before. My name is Ryan Kinnley," he said as he stretched out his hand.

"Aaron... no we haven't met."

"What happened to ya? You look like you've had a rough day, you okay?"

"You could say that, but it would be an understatement," Aaron said with a grin, he couldn't help himself, Ryan was just looking at him as if it was completely normal to run into someone caked in mud and looking like they had just been through a hurricane.

"Anything I could do to help?"

"Thanks but I need to get home, it's been a long day and I really need a shower."

"Well, you need a ride? I could drive you, it's pretty wet outside, or maybe you already knew that," he said with that lopsided smile again.

"Sure, I'd really appreciate that. Is it raining? I hadn't noticed." With that both boys laughed all the way to Ryan's navy blue pickup truck. Aaron had never met someone that he "clicked with" so well.

Aaron discovered that there was a youth group on Tuesday's at 7:00 PM, a communion service on Wednesday's at 7:30 PM, and a Sunday morning service at 9:00 and 11:00 AM. He also found out that Ryan coaches a little league soccer team for six to eight year olds, helps with a monthly food drive, and helps organize fund raisers for the children's ministry.

"I asked what you did for fun," Aaron stated astonished.

"It *is* fun, you ever tried it?"

"Well, no, but what I meant was, what you do with your friends that's all."

"My friends do all that stuff with me," he said smiling at Aaron. "I know God wants me to help in whatever way I can, so I try to do my best, and in the end I always end up having a blast."

"Really?" Aaron was astonished, "I mean... that's great." Aaron was starting to think his new friend might be a couple fries short of a happy meal but he liked that in a person. As they pulled in front of Aaron's brick colonial Ryan asked, "So am I going to see you tomorrow? Youth group seven o'clock?"

"Ya, I'll be there, thanks for the ride. I'll see ya." Aaron wasn't sure about going, but decided he would keep the idea open in his mind.

Aaron watched Ryan pull away and waved before he headed up to the front door. He was worried his parents would still be home so he snuck in quietly, and hurried right up to his room. He decided Mack would have to wait just a little while longer for a call back because a shower was definitely a priority.

When he was clean and dressed he ran downstairs to see if his mom was home and when she wasn't, he grabbed a bag of Doritos and a Coke and headed back to his room to call Mack.

"Hey Mack, so you're not mad at me anymore?"

"I never said that, just wanted to know what you were up to."

"Look I'm sorry about today, I didn't mean to be that way, you have no idea what kind of day I've had and you kind of caught me right after I found out what my grade was in history."

"Dang, didn't you study for that last test?"

"I did, but that B+ I made on that test didn't do much to help."

"Are you going to get grounded again? How bad is it?"

"A D but if I get that extra credit in and ace my last two tests I might pull a B-."

"Well, you better because we're supposed to hang out this weekend, that new bowling alley opens up Friday."

"I didn't forget and you're on, I hope you have been practicing."

"Against you I don't need to… anyway you said you had a bad day, what else happened?"

"Other than not eating all day, I ran into Gus and his two goons after school."

"Those jerks, what did they say to you?"

"They did more than say this time."

"Aaron, what happened?"

"Gus and I started fighting and when I started to win Paul and Teddy jumped in, they really messed me up. I have a bruise on my thigh and side the size of a football and a huge bump on the back of my head, I have no idea how that happened but the Tylenol I took isn't doing a thing for my head," Aaron recounted.

"Man I wish I was bigger."

"Don't you do a thing, they don't mess with you and I'd like to keep it that way."

"Can I least send 'em a couple hundred viruses so they can't use their computer for at least a month?" Aaron had to smile at his friends ingenuity, Mack was the only person he knew of that could break into the banks e-mail system and is completely self taught.

"Now *that* you can do, I am going to get going though. I want to get on the computer for a bit before I start on that extra credit."

"Alright, I'll see ya after first hour then."

Aaron looked around his room at the posters of athletes, his TV, and his computer until he saw his reflection in the full length mirror on the inside of his bedroom door and stared intently at himself. He wondered what it was about him that those kids at school took exception to. Was it his wavy almost black hair, olive colored skin, or maybe his overly large sea green eyes? His eyes he thought, my dad must have these eyes. His mom always used to tell him that angel's must have kissed his eyes because she had never met anyone with his particular shade of green. He couldn't notice anything else particularly out of the ordinary; he was an average size for a boy of fifteen. He had started using his step dads' weights and doing exercises when the trouble started with Gus so that he could at least try to stand up for himself. Aaron never wanted his mom to know what was happening at school. She has enough to worry about, Aaron would tell himself, without worrying about him. His full, girl-looking lips troubled him though. He smiled to himself as he remembered asking Mack if there was such a thing as a lip reduction in plastic surgery, and Mack died laughing saying 'what *lip*osuction?' They laughed so hard they were both holding there sides when they recovered.

"Oh well, it doesn't matter what they don't like about me, I can't change anything anyway," he said to his image in the mirror.

~3~

*'If one falls down, his friend can help him up.
But pity the man who has no one....'*
Ecclesiastes 4:10(NIV)

Aaron awoke to his mom screeching at him from her bedroom down the hall that he was going to be late for school. He jumped out of bed and threw on a clean pair of faded jeans, T-shirt and his favorite Red Wings cap. He dashed to the bathroom quickly brushed his teeth and dashed out the door yelling 'love ya mom' as he slammed the door behind himself. He sprinted the five blocks to school and made it with four minutes to spare.

Aaron waited at their usual spot after first period for Mack. He saw the long curly red hair first, then her big goofy smile when she noticed him. She was wearing slightly flared low rider jeans and a black hoodie.
"Hey brat."
"Hey yourself, have you seen Gus yet?"
"No, and I really hope I don't today, I think I have had enough of that kid to last me a month."
Mackenzie Ashton stared up at Aaron with her large green-blue eyes and smiled as she said, "I agree. Well he is one boy that won't

be using his computer for a while." She smiled innocently up at him as he raised an eyebrow. "I emailed him a computer virus that's the equivalent of the Ebola virus ten times over."

"How do you know that he'll open it?"

"I opened a guest account on my server and said I was a secret admirer... he will open it." Aaron smiled to himself at her cleverness.

"You look like crap. Did you get those scratches from yesterday? The wuss scratched you didn't he?"

"Yeah, I almost thought I was fighting a girl."

"Hey watch it now, I'll show you how a girl fights," Mackenzie laughed out.

"I don't consider you a girl." Aaron knew he was provoking her but it was too much fun.

"What is that supposed to mean?" she said as she socked him in the shoulder.

"Well any girl that plays street hockey, steals my clothes whenever she comes over, can out run and out do every one in the school including the guys in the phys ed championship for push-ups isn't a chick in my book."

"Don't over exaggerate, I only took two of your sweatshirts and you know the Red Wings are my favorite, so you should have hidden them when you knew I was coming over. And so what if the guys in this school are wimps, I can't help that," she couldn't help but be proud of her quick come back and her grin said as much.

"I was sick that day, so let's not label *all* the guys in school as wimps."

"I'll take you on any time."

"You're on. We better go or you'll be getting a detention from Mrs. Warbner."

"Man you're right, see ya." With that she started off down the hall.

At lunch Aaron scanned the cafeteria for Justin and spotted him sitting with Mike, Ralph, and Tracey. He grabbed a pop and some chips from the vending machine and made his way over to their table.

"What's up Aaron?" Ralph asked. Ralph Dragner was a tall brown haired boy with brown eyes. He and Aaron had known each other since the seventh grade. They had been best friends for a while when they first met but Ralph had started hanging out with his cousins more when they were in eighth grade and now they saw each other at lunch and occasionally on the weekends if they ended up at the same place.

"Hey dude," Mike said without even looking up. Mike Dirvine was the class clown, always goofing around and cracking jokes. He and Aaron had been friends since about sixth grade when he was transferred here from Cleveland, Ohio.

"Hey guys," Aaron returned.

"What happened to you yesterday? I waited for you for like a half hour and then left," Justin March said in-between mouthfuls. He was scarfing down today's special 'fiestada' which is kind of like a pizza but it's in the shape of an octagon, has cheddar cheese and some kind of brown sauce with chunks of hamburger in it to replace what should be pizza sauce. Watching Justin drenching it in ranch dressing and taking bites almost too large for him to chew made Aaron rethink where he sat down for lunch.

"Sorry about that, something came up."

"How you been, Aaron?" Tracy Carter asked. "I haven't seen you around in a while."

Rumor has it that the short brown haired girl with hazel-eyes that dresses a bit too hippy has had a crush on Aaron since the beginning of the school year. But Aaron's never been one to give much credit to the rumor weed. "Not to bad, how about you?"

"Same I guess, you going to be at the wrestling match on Friday? I'll save you a seat."

"Not this time, I have some things to do." Aaron replied remembering he had plans to go with Mack to the bowling alley.

"Well, I'll save you a seat in case you change your mind."

"Thanks, I'll see what I can do." She smiled shyly at him before turning her attention back to Wendy Berry who was now seated next to her.

Aaron was pleased that he made it through the rest of the day without running into Gus. He was staring intently at the clock counting down the seconds for the final bell to ring. He was more than ready when the annoyingly loud buzz sounded over the intercom. He joined the stampede in the hall way and was surprised to find Mack waiting for him by the exit. "Hey, I thought you had something going on after school."

"It wasn't that important, I was just going to reload my computers, it can wait. I'd rather hang out with you. You busy?"

"Nope, not until later, what do you want to do?" Aaron asked.

"Go to my house and pig out, I'm starving. What are you doing later?"

"Hanging out with this kid Ryan, you don't know him."

"Oh, where do you know him from?"

"Just a kid I met the other day, he hooked me up with a ride when it was raining out." Aaron didn't know how Mack would react to him going to church and wasn't even sure he was going to keep his promise to go so he decided not to mention it.

"You ready to jet?"

"Yup, let me just grab my dang history book."

The two friends sat at Mackenzie's kitchen table eating potato chips and dip, laughing as Aaron recited the story about Gus at the doctor's and how Paul and Teddy reacted when they heard it.

"I had the dream again," Aaron sobered.

"Was it the same one or was it different this time?"

"It was a bit different, it's weird when I see myself in the dreams I always get the same feeling, but they are always either different in where we are or what's going on."

"Tell me."

"This time I was under water but I didn't need to breathe. My dad was with me but I still couldn't see his face. There were the most beautiful creatures and fish around us, some as big as a house but I never felt afraid. My dad and I were swimming together and I never felt so complete and... safe."

"Wow, that's amazing, I just wish we knew what all these dreams meant. I mean you have to be having them for a reason."

"Maybe it means I need to find my dad or I'll never feel complete."

"Why don't you look for him Aaron, what's the worse that can happen?"

"What's the worse that can happen? He could tell me he hates me, or that he doesn't want anything to do with me, or that he didn't want to be found." He finished while staring attentively at his hands.

"Aaron, you know as well as I do that not knowing has been eating you up inside. If you don't try to find him you will never know the truth."

"You're right, I have been doing this for way too long, and I don't think I can live the rest of my life without knowing why he left. Will you help me? I don't have much to go on."

"Are you kidding me? Of course I am going to help, actually, don't be mad but I have been looking for him for the last few months. I paid one of those 'Find a Friend' companies to look with that birthday money I had been sitting on but they haven't come up with anything just yet, they have some leads though."

"What?!? Mack how could you do that and not tell me? What would you have done if they found him?" Aaron said in complete shock, his mind reeling with the possibility that his father could actually be found any day now.

"Well, I would have told you and you would have either decided to talk to him or not. Aaron, I was trying to do a good thing, I knew one day you would decide to look for him."

"What information did you give them, I mean how did you?" Aaron was having a hard time speaking, his stomach turned as the thought of actually talking to his father became a reality instead of a fantasy.

"I know you have that box with all the stuff your mom gave you. I told them his name and gave them that address in there from 1990. That's all they really needed to start." Mackenzie smiled reassuringly at her friend.

Aaron stared at the ceramic tile not knowing how to react. He was upset that she would take it upon herself to do something that was so personal to him and at the same time was amazed at the lengths she went to.

As Aaron embraced his best friend he whispered, "Thank you, I don't know what I would do without you."

~4~

'But because of His great love for us, God who is rich in mercy, made us alive with Christ even when we were dead in transgressions – It is by grace you have been saved.'
Ephesians 2:4, 5 (NIV)

Aaron left Mack's house about 6:30 and headed towards the church. He didn't know why he was even going, but figured he had nothing else to do. He was kind of nervous, he would only know one person there and he had no idea what a youth group was all about. When he arrived he stared at the big double doors observing the throngs of kids walking in. He recognized some of them from school but no one he had ever talked to before. It was ten to seven when he walked into the church. He only hoped Ryan was there already.

Aaron stood in the entry way watching the mass of kids swarm into the sanctuary, there appeared to be kids as young as eleven and as old as eighteen. He received some smiles, and hellos from the friendly attendees and two youth pastors. Aaron grew anxious to find Ryan and decided he should look around in the sanctuary before the entry way was completely empty and all the people were seated. Aaron followed a giggly group of twelve year old girls into the sanctuary and immediately saw Ryan standing in the front row talking to two older boys. Ryan noticed Aaron soon after he arrived in the sanctuary standing by the doors looking like a deer caught in headlights.

Aaron was relieved when he saw Ryan wave him over and felt even more at ease when he saw the two older boys Ryan was with smile and wave him over as well. He was surprised to receive a hug from Ryan before an introduction to the two other boys, Jake and Billy. Ryan showed him the spot he had reserved for Aaron next to him in the front row, Aaron sat down wishing he wasn't so close to the front. He had never sat in the front row at school, and really didn't want to start doing it now.

As Aaron looked around the room he was amazed at the turn out, there was well over fifty youth in attendance. He turned his attention to the stage and saw the choir filing in with the band, and what he assumed were the pastors take there spots to the left of the stage. He felt a tinge of anxiety but decided to wait it out.

The music began and every one stood up in unison except for Aaron who quickly followed suit. Aaron gave a quick glance up at Ryan to see if he noticed and gave a sheepish grin when he saw Ryan looking at him with his lopsided grin then elbowed him in the side. The music was just as remarkable as the day before but more upbeat. Aaron was taken aback by the enthusiasm of the young crowd. Kids were clapping, dancing, singing with all their hearts and raising their hands as the music played. Surprisingly, he didn't feel awkward and decided to just listen to the words of the song.
"My Jesus, my Redeemer, Lord nothing compares to you. All of my life, all that I need is Your everlasting peace. I need You, I love You, and all that You are is what I desire to be. Why struggle, why stumble, when You offer a life of joy and redemption."
Aaron couldn't help but get excited over the music, he couldn't

explain it but it was like his whole body responded to the words and he couldn't help but smile, even if he didn't want to he couldn't contain it, he felt joy, *real joy.*

After a few more songs the choir stopped singing and the whole room sat down except for one man on stage that couldn't have been more than 26 years old. Dressed in a pair of khakis and a Polo shirt, he walked over to the podium equipped with a microphone in the center of the stage.

"How is everyone tonight," the man asked enthusiastically, to the crowds resounding cheer.

"For those of you who don't know me already, my name is Pastor John and I'm so excited to be here tonight, God is good isn't he." Again the crowd of teens applauded.

"Let's open up tonight with prayer. Dear Lord, we thank You for this day, and ask that You would give us the ears to hear what the Spirit is speaking to us. We are so grateful for everything You are doing in the church and in our lives. Let Your truth sink into our hearts and guide us in our lives. We thank You for Your blessings and rejoice in You always, in Jesus' name, Amen."

"I really feel that God is moving right now in the hearts and lives of our youth," he was answered with another passionate cheer of the crowd. "The Lord has placed upon my heart to speak again tonight about God's promises to us and what living in covenant with Him means. God promises us that if we believe in Him and that His Son died for our sins and was raised again and confess it with our mouths that we shall not perish but have everlasting life. But do you know that there is so much more He wants for us than that?"

Aaron listened as Pastor John spoke of living a life of peace and joy, of never having to worry about failure because walking on God's path instead of the worlds meant that even if we fail He will be there to pick up the pieces for us. He spoke of God's love and how He gave to us first by giving His Son so that we might live. He talked about what Jesus went through and why He did what He did and that once we accept the Lord He would never ever leave us. The young pastor wept as he told the teens about the degradation, the crown of thorns, the beating, the whipping, and finally the cross. Pastor John said that even though Jesus went through all of the temptations we do every day, He never sinned, He was blameless and still He paid for every sin we may commit.

Aaron tried to hold back his tears and truly had no idea why he would be getting so emotional but failed miserably in his efforts as big teardrops slid down his face. He felt Ryan's hand on his shoulder and was somehow comforted by it. Aaron wanted to believe in all that the pastor was saying; something inside him needed it to be true.

There was a struggle inside Aaron as he gave all the reasons why it couldn't be true. 'I'm supposed to believe in bedtime stories now? How can anyone believe so strongly in something they can't see? Even if it was true what have I ever done to deserve all that? If my own dad didn't love me enough to stick around no one else ever will. I must have been nuts to even come here,' he told himself. But still there was a spark of hope that he *was* worth it to someone, anyone, that he could be loved like that was a dream he never thought he could achieve. Everything inside him wanted it to be real.

"The Lord wants me to have an alter call for anyone here who is ready to ask the Lord into their lives. If you haven't made the decision yet for God and are ready to make your commitment to Him please come up to the front."

Aaron watched four young teens walk unsteadily with tear streaked faces towards the stairs of the stage, as the youth leaders on stage met them at the base of the stairs and laid their hands on the shaky teens while whispering to them.

Just then Pastor John said, "There's someone here who is struggling within themselves and the Lord wants you to know that no one deserves His gift to us, that is what His mercy is all about, and that you are worth it to Him, He has been waiting for you for so long and He wants You to come to Him now, because You belong to Him, you always have."

Aaron couldn't believe what he was hearing, he felt the words were just for him and was in awe of the emotions welling up inside of him. As Pastor John spoke Aaron felt the presence of something so much bigger than himself all around him and in him. He felt as though he was being hugged on the inside, there was no shame anymore. He didn't care who was there or what they thought. Aaron's whole body racked with sobs until he couldn't sit upright anymore, it was as if something inside of him realized he was in the actual presence of God and he couldn't get low enough to the ground. The next thing he was conscious of was lying flat on the carpet with at least five or six sets of hands on him, and voices coaxing and encouraging him to say what he so desperately needed to.

"I'm so sorry, I am so sorry," is all that could come out of Aaron's quivering lips. He was so sorry for not knowing sooner that God was there, sorry for doubting what was true, sorry for every mistake he had ever made. Still the voices were there telling him that God had already forgiven him, and all he needed to do was to confess it with his mouth.

"I believe in You… I believe that You sent Your son to die for me… I believe that I am a sinner and that Jesus died for my sins… I believe… I believe that Jesus rose from the dead so that I might live. I am so sorry, I don't deserve this, I don't deserve You." Aaron suddenly felt as though the squeezing in his heart eased and he felt a peace like he had never experienced before.

He raised himself to his knees and when he opened his eyes was stunned to see every person that was with him had been crying as well. Pastor John hugged him before returning to the podium to dismiss everyone. Ryan, Jake and Billy stayed with him kneeling down in front of their chairs. The youth leaders who had obviously finished with the initial four who went to the altar, smiled at him and then followed Pastor John to the stage.

Aaron stared at the three young men who remained with him and said, "I can't believe what just happened, I feel like I'm not the same person anymore."

"You're not, you've been reborn," Billy remarked.

"It was like I fainted but was still awake, why did I fall like that?"

"Because you were in the presence of the almighty God and His presence is so awesome that your natural body couldn't be there without showing reverence to Him," Ryan responded.

"Wow… that was so unbelievable! My whole body is still shaking. Does God come like that a lot? Does this happen all the time?"

"God's presence can come in many ways. You may feel joy, or an unbelievable peace, or you may feel so overwhelmed you just stand there and cry and you know it's because He's so close to you and He loves you. Don't get caught up in the feeling of Him though because that's a real hard lesson I just learned, He is not just a feeling, and just because you don't feel anything doesn't mean He's not there."

"Does He talk to you? Like can you actually hear Him?"

"He speaks to us in lots of ways. This kind of experience is just one way God speaks. He spoke to you through Pastor John. He also talks to your heart when you pray, and you just know it was Him. He can talk to you in an audible voice although I have never heard Him that way, through other people, through situations, and also dreams and visions. He speaks to each person differently."

Just then Jake touched Aaron's shoulder and said, "I just wanted you to know that I am so grateful right now for being a part of that," and with that Jake and Billy left. Ryan helped Aaron to his feet and embraced him.

"He's got you now, and He'll never let you go."

"I'm counting on that, I feel like anything is possible right now."
"Anything is… with God."

They talked about God and what had happened as Ryan drove Aaron home. Before Ryan left he and Aaron exchanged numbers and Ryan made him promise that he would be at church the following night for the communion service.

Aaron didn't think he would be able to sleep at all, but when he crawled into bed that night he slept better then he ever had.

****

7:30 couldn't come soon enough for Aaron. He had so much anticipation he could hardly stand it. He felt like a child waiting for Christmas morning. I must be losing my mind Aaron thought to himself.

Aaron ran into Mack after school.
"Why are you in such a good mood?" Mack questioned.
"So far it's been a good day."
"Well, at least one of us has. Anyway, what are you doing tonight?"
"Hanging out with Ryan, that kid I told you about." Aaron answered.
"What's up with him? Why are you hanging out with him a lot all of a sudden?" she asked.
"Nothing, just a new friend, he's pretty cool."
"Maybe I could hang with you guys."
"No! I mean why? He doesn't come to our school or anything," Aaron's voice rose by at least two octaves.
"Alright, I have a hockey game tonight so I'll talk to you tomorrow."
"Ok, good luck," Aaron said trying to get off the subject.

"See you tomorrow," Mack replied.
With that they went their separate ways.

Aaron was lying on his bed staring at the ceiling when his mom called him for dinner.

"I made your favorite, lasagna. Is something wrong hunny?" Aaron's mom asked as her inquisitive gaze turned into a scrutinizing one. "What happened to your face, you have scratches all over?"
"Nothings wrong I was just playing basketball with the guys." Aaron didn't want this to turn into another one of her four hour interrogations. He loved his mom and the last thing he wanted for her was to worry. He had no idea how she would react to him getting into a fight and figured it would be much better for everyone if he just kept it to himself.

"Did you spray Bactine on it? You know you can get an infection and get scars on your face." Most kids can't stand it when their parents tell them the same things over and over like they are six again, but Aaron knew his mom only did it because she loved him and that is just one of her ways of showing it. Aaron just smiled and nodded as he settled into his chair at the kitchen table.

"So how was your day at school Aaron?" His step-father asked. His step-dad was tall with brown hair and eyes. Aaron liked the guy, he's been around since Aaron was eight years old and he seemed to make his mom happy but there just wasn't a real father-son spark there, maybe it was Aaron's fault he thought, it really didn't matter.
"Ok I guess. I turned in my extra credit assignment for History class." Aaron replied.
"Great, you think that'll help pull your grade up a bit?"
"That's what Mr. Brisby said."
"Well, every little bit helps."

Aaron watched his parents exchange goofy smiles as they started eating.

"Could you pass me the parmesan Beth?" Ben asked his wife.

Beth passed it with a wink and Aaron thought he was going to be ill. His mom and step-dad always did stuff like that and Aaron thought they were losing their minds. They *are* married after all, isn't all that flirty dating stuff suppose to stop?

Aaron cleared the table and helped with the dishes after dinner. He turned down his moms offer for him to join them in watching some old war movie they rented at the video store.

"You know there's more to life than video games and James Bond shoot outs. You might learn something if you watch with us." His mom's intentions were good but Aaron just couldn't give in tonight, he wanted to get ready for church.

"I know mom, I am rotting my brain and believe me next time you got some thirty year old movie you want me to watch I will. I've just got some stuff to do."

"Alright, but I won't let you tell me no next time."

"I know you won't, believe me." Aaron gave his last comment over his shoulder as he headed up to his room.

Aaron arrived at the church twenty minutes early and reserved a few seats in the front row for Ryan, himself, Billy and Jake. It wasn't long before Ryan arrived and took his seat next to Aaron and the two talked until Jake and Billy sat down just before the service started. The sanctuary was full to standing room only in no time.

The pastor was different than last night; he was older maybe in his late forties and dressed in a nice suit. He spoke about our burdens and that the bible teaches us that God's burden is light and when things get to hard we should be giving the problems to God and trust Him to deal with them. Aaron thought about his dad and how he has been carrying so much guilt, confusion and torment over not knowing him or why he left.

THE ONLY WAY HOME

"Lord, I'm not sure how to do this, but I need you to help me in my search to find my father, I know I will never feel complete unless I find him. I need to know who he is so I can find out who I am. I am giving You this problem of mine because I know that's what You want me to do, I have faith in You and I won't worry about this anymore," Aaron prayed. Aaron immediately felt like a weight had been lifted from his shoulders.

When he got home that night his mom informed him that Mack had called at least three times. Aaron called her back from his room and she answered it half way through the first ring.
"Aaron!"
"What's going on?"
"You won't believe it, that company I hired called me this afternoon... Aaron... they gave me the phone number."

~5~

'Look at the birds of the air; they do not sow or reap or store away in barns, and yet your heavenly Father feeds them. Are you not much more valuable then they? Who of you by worrying can add a single hour to his life?'
Matthew 6:26, 27 (NIV)

"Phone number?"

"Your dad's number… to call him!" Mack exclaimed with an uncontainable enthusiasm.

"They called you and gave you my dad's home telephone number? How do they know it's his?"

"I guess from a utility bill. It doesn't matter anyway does it?" Mack waited for a response from Aaron but there was only silence at the other end of the line. "Are you ok? Aaron this is it, this is what you wanted right? Now you can find out what happened."

"This is what I wanted but I guess now that I have it I don't know if I really did… maybe not knowing is better. I mean if you think about it Mack he left me, maybe he doesn't want to be found. What the heck am I suppose to say to him?" Aaron was becoming more confused and tense by the moment.

"Aaron, deep breaths… don't freak out on me. I thought you would be happy, I'm sorry, maybe this was a bad idea."

"Don't you dare apologize! Thank you so much for this. I'm just not sure what to do now… I mean what *do* you say to your dad that you don't even remember meeting?"

"What you do now is call him. Get it over with Aaron, how bad can it be really? The worst case scenario is that he hangs up on you then you know what the truth is."

"And what would the truth be then?"

"That he's a bum and he doesn't deserve a kid like you."

"Well, thanks for that anyway. Will you come over after school tomorrow and we'll call together?"

"I think I'd have to kill you if you called and I wasn't there, I'll meet you right after sixth hour by the doors, okay?"

"Alright see you tomorrow, night."

"Night."

Aaron sat on the floor of his room trying to think of the perfect thing to say to his dad tomorrow but the best he could come up with was 'Hello… you may not remember me but…' It was pathetic but what else could he say?

****

Aaron couldn't remember the last time he had butterflies in his stomach but he had them all day and at lunch he thought if he even put one bite of food into his mouth it wasn't going to stay down. Mack was supportive when he saw her but he couldn't help but feel like she just didn't understand.

"Aaron, you need to lighten up a bit, it's not going to be that bad. You're just going to call him."

"Just going to call him!?! This is like the biggest day of my life and you're telling me to *'lighten up'*!" Aaron could not control his rising temper, but he did try. "I'm sorry, I really am trying to mellow out but it's hard, actually the hardest thing I've ever done. I just need to be alone for a while. I'm sorry Mack. I'll see you after school."

Mack knew her friend well enough to know when to back off. Aaron is the greatest friend she has ever had, but he can be quick to fly off the handle. Mack tried not to get hurt by him because she knew he wasn't actually mad at her, but sometimes it was hard to do.

"Don't worry, it'll be ok. I'll see you later," she managed with the best smile she could muster, and turned to head to her next class.

Aaron was feeling like a jerk as he waited by the doors for Mack after the final bell rang. 'I can be such a jerk,' he thought to himself. He knew he had hurt her feelings but he just couldn't help it, he felt so anxious and he was hungry to top it off. She was smiling at him when he noticed her coming towards him. 'If I were her I wouldn't be smiling,' he thought. 'I don't deserve a friend like her, she found my dad for me, paid for it even and all I have done is growled at her because she doesn't understand what I am going through. Nice friend I am.'

"Hey ugly," Mack challenged being her usual bubbly self.

Aaron raised an eyebrow at that, but was happy she was obviously back to normal.

"What's up freak?" was his pathetic comeback.

"I'm glad you're doing better."

"Yeah I am, sorry about earlier today. I didn't mean to be a jerk." Her reply was a grin.

They laughed most of the way to Aaron's house but when they arrived Aaron's butterflies came back with a vengeance. Mack noticed Aaron's face pale as they grabbed some snacks and sat down at the table.

"Are you going to be ok?"

"I will, lets just get this over with."

Mack pulled a paper out of her back pack with the telephone number and address of Tony Guarez written on it.

"So where does my dad live?"
"Fort Worth, Texas."
"That's a long way from here. I've never been to Texas."
"Me either... you ready to do this?"
"I don't think you are ever ready for something like this."

Aaron took the paper from Mackenzie and picked up the phone and then quickly set it back on the receiver again.

"Will you call the first time and just see if he's home then hang up?"
"If you want me to I will."

Aaron handed Mackenzie the phone and she quickly dialed. He watched as her face lit up a couple seconds later and then hung up.

"I take it he was home."

"Yep!" Mack couldn't help it, she was so excited she could barely sit still.

"Ok I'll call, but what do I say?"
"How about 'hi, remember me?'"

Aaron grinned at her and reached for the phone again. He dialed the number and then pressed the phone to his ear. He heard a man's voice answer and he just sat there, paralyzed. He heard him say hello again and he couldn't speak, he wanted to, he even opened his mouth but no words came. The man hung up and Aaron just sat there with the phone to his ear.

"Aaron? You ok?"

"I couldn't do it." Aaron held back tears. He didn't want to cry in front of her.

"You can do it Aaron, I know you can. How long have you been waiting for this moment? I know it's hard but think about when this first part is over with, you will know what happened, why he left and hasn't been here for you and more importantly whether or not he wants to now."

Aaron stared at her as a single tear streamed down his cheek and then he reached for the phone again.

"Hello!?"

"Yes umm… are you Tony Guarez?"

"No man, he moved about a week ago."

Aaron felt numb as his hopes started to slide away from him.

"You still there?"

"Sorry, I'm here still."

"Well, you want his new address? He don't got a phone turned on yet but I got the address of where he's supposed to be at."

"Yeah sure, please." Aaron grabbed the notebook out of Mack's bag and scribbled the new address down.

"Hey thanks, I appreciate it."

"No prob, take it easy."

"You too." Aaron hung up the phone and looked at Mack who was now pacing the kitchen.

"So what happened? Obviously he wasn't home, what's the address for?"

"He moved last week, this is his new address."

Mack grabbed the notebook, "He moved to Pensacola, Florida last week? So where's the phone number?"

"There isn't one because he just moved, and he doesn't have it turned on yet I guess."

"Well, you can just call this guy back in like a week or so and get it then."

"I guess so."

Aaron felt completely deflated and somehow relieved at the same time.

Aaron called Ryan after Mack left because he didn't know anyone else who would be able to give him guidance on what to do with how he feels.

"Hey Ryan."

"Aaron, how are you?"

"I'm alright, you?"

"Good here, you sure you are ok? You sound down."

"Well, alright is kind of a generic answer, nobody says crappy… how about you?"

"True, so what's going on?"

Aaron explained about his dad and how he had given the situation to God at church yesterday and when he got home that night his friend had called and they had gotten his number. He told him the events of the day and that he didn't understand why God would give him the number if he wasn't living there anymore.

"I feel like I am unraveling from the inside out," Aaron muttered. "I don't know what I am supposed to do here. Part of me feels like why am I even looking, another part says I can't even wait a week to talk to him, and the last part feels like a dumb phone call will never be enough."

"You asked God to take the burden from you and deal with it. If you believe it was Him who gave you the number maybe He's just giving you a lesson on patience because you have to wait a little while to talk to your dad."

"I hadn't thought of that, but even if that's true how am I supposed to feel?"

"You already said you gave it to God, maybe you need to do that again and ask Him for direction."

"Oh and what's He going to do slip a note under my bedroom door to let me know?"

"When He talks to you, you'll know. The key is being quiet enough inside of yourself to hear it."

"Quiet enough inside, what's that suppose to mean?"

"It means instead of worrying about it, calm yourself down because you know God is working it out for you, trust him and just listen."

"I don't know if I can, I guess I'll just do my best and keep praying."

"It's going to be alright, you got the Big Guy on your side this time and He won't let you down."

"Thanks, I'm sure I'll feel better tomorrow. I have to go; it's getting late, thanks Ryan."

"Hey anytime, talk to you soon."

~6~

'In the last days, God says, I will pour out my spirit on all people. Your sons and daughters will prophecy, your young men will see visions, your old men will dream dreams.'
Acts 2:17 (NIV)

Aaron feigned sickness as his mom tried to find the thermometer. He had too much on his mind to try and think at school.

"I can never find the dang thermometer when I need it; I swear I have bought at least five of those things. Are you sure you will be okay by yourself? I just can't miss a day of work right now because of our trip." Aaron's mom and step-dad were leaving town for a week to go to Las Vegas for Ben's sisters wedding.

"Mom, I'm fifteen now you know, I think I can manage. I will make myself soup for lunch and take Tylenol and everything." Aaron wasn't normally sarcastic with his mom but he just wanted her to leave so he could think.

"Okay, okay, I just worry about you. I know you aren't a baby anymore, forgive me for wanting to hold onto the thought that you still need me sometimes."

"I do need you mom, and I love you too. I just don't feel good, I'm sorry for being like that."

"Don't worry, I'll call at lunch and make sure you are doing alright. If you need me you know my work number right?"

"Yes, mom." She smiled at him, kissed his forehead and shuffled out of the room.

Aaron waited until he heard the garage open and close signifying his mom's departure before he got on his knees and started to pray.

"Lord, I know I have already prayed about this, but I'm just so confused and I need to know what I should do… I need You to tell me what I should do because I am completely lost on this one. I give this to You, in Jesus name, amen." Aaron wasn't feeling much better as he stood up to go downstairs for some breakfast.

As he walked past his mom and Ben's room he heard a voice saying, "Ask and it will be given to you; seek and you will find; knock and the door will be opened to you. For everyone who asks receives; he who seeks finds; and to him who knocks, the door will be opened. That was from Matthew chapter seven verses seven and eight. This is another scripture for our topic today; 'seeking the Father'." Aaron stopped cold in his tracks and opened his mother's bedroom door to see that the television was left on and a pastor was speaking.

"That had to have been an answer, God wants me to go and seek after my father and if I knock the door will open to me!" Aaron hadn't skipped since he was six or seven years old but he skipped all the way to the kitchen to pour a bowl of Sugar Smacks. He sat at the table eating as a very uneasy feeling came over him. He couldn't pin point the cause of it, but it was definitely real. He figured that he had to work on trusting in God and tried to not let it ruin his enthusiasm. Aaron looked up the number to the Greyhound station and called to see how much it would cost to get to Florida from Michigan.

He watched about as much day time T.V. as he could before falling fast asleep on the couch. Aaron dreamt that he was standing in the middle of the desert, his face burnt from the sun. He could taste the salt from his sweat on his lips and tried to peel some of the clothes he was wearing off of his damp body to try and relieve himself from the unbearable heat. As he pulled his shirt off he felt the sun's rays sting his flesh and so he put it back on deciding the intense heat was better than the searing pain of the sun on his skin. He found it hard to breathe as he looked around for somewhere to go, somewhere to escape the excruciating conditions. There was nothing.

Everywhere he looked was brownish red sand, not even a tree to try and shade himself. He started walking, searching for a place to find refuge and as he made it to the top of a sand dune he saw a cluster of trees with a shallow pond in the center. He estimated the oasis to be only a half mile away as he started towards it. He licked his lips and felt their cracked dryness and couldn't even produce enough spit to wet them. His throat burned in protest as he started to run towards his shelter. As he neared the edge of the trees he let out a sigh of relief that he had made it and used his last bit of energy to lunge straight into the water. He felt his body hit coarse sand instead of the cool dampness of the water and realized nothing was there. He looked around in disbelief and again saw only the sand and only felt the dryness and the scorching heat. He was despaired and felt betrayed by his own mind at believing in the mirage. He curled into a ball in the sand and started to sob.

Aaron awoke to the annoying buzz of his door bell, he shook trying to pull himself out of the dream but he was still trying to wet his lips. He had never had a dream seem so real before. He quickly stood to his feet and hurried to the front door, his body still trembling. He wasn't too surprised to see Mack standing there.

"What took you so long? I rang the door bell like seven times?" She said disgruntled as she stepped into the entry way.

"Sorry, I fell asleep on the couch watching T.V.," Aaron noticed

Mackenzie's younger brother Maxwell trailing behind her, he ran after the six year old pretending to be a monster.

"What happened to you today? Why weren't you at school?" She questioned after the two calmed down.

"I didn't feel like it today so I told my mom I was sick. Hey Max, you want to go up and play some video games in my room?" The youngster didn't need any more coaxing than that and he bounded up the stairs as he had done several times before.

"Ah, well what's going on? Are you doing better with this whole dad thing?" Mack asked obviously concerned about him.

"Actually I am doing great! I have decided that I am going to go to Pensacola and see my dad face to face instead of calling him," Aaron said with certainty and a grin.

"*What*? Are you nuts? Florida is on the other side of the country how do you suppose you are going to get your mom to be ok with you going there?"

"I'm not, she's going out of town with Ben a week from tomorrow for his sisters' wedding and I am supposed to be staying at Justin's house, but I am going to Florida instead."

"You are serious aren't you?"

"Yep, I am going to go to Greyhound and buy the ticket, its $169.00 round trip and I have $423.00 in my drawer upstairs from mowing lawns all last summer. I have more in the bank but I could go with just that. I figure it takes one day to get there, another to get back, and maybe a couple days there; so four or five days total I'll be gone."

"Well, if you are going, I am too."

"Are *you* nuts now?"

"No, I *am* going though. You aren't going to Florida without me. Besides my cousin and her friend took a Greyhound last month from Chicago to here for a visit and I found out that friends travel free!"

"*What*?"

"Greyhound lets you bring a friend for free."

"Are you sure?"

"Do I look like I'm kidding? So you book the trip for both of us and we can split the cost of the bus."

"No way, you aren't going, you will get in so much trouble it's not even funny."

"I can say I am going to go to Sylvie's for the week and she will cover for me, my parents have been bugging me to go see her, and with the two day week we have in school that week, they won't care."

"I forgot about that, we only have school Thursday and Friday that week."

"So it will be perfect."

"I really don't think this is a good idea Mack, this is something *I* need to do, not you. It's stupid for you to risk being grounded until you are thirty when this doesn't even matter to you."

"You really are an idiot aren't you? This *is* important to me because you are my best friend. You have no idea what's going to happen when you get there and I *want* to be there with you. My mind is made up Aaron McKay, I am going!"

~7~

'Ask the former generations and find out what their fathers learned, for we were born only yesterday and know nothing, and our days on earth are but a shadow. Will they not instruct you and tell you? Will they not bring forth words from their understanding?'
Job 8:8, 9, 10 (NIV)

"Well, don't blame me when you get nailed for this."

"I won't. I am going to go home and figure out how to make this fool proof. So, I'll meet you at seven at Sonny Lanes right?"

"I'll be there."

"See you, and don't say anything to *anyone*, seriously, no one."

"Gotcha, don't worry." Mack grabbed her things, called for her brother and headed out the door without a glance back. Aaron knew better than to argue with her anymore, his only hope was that her alibi would some how fall through. The last thing Aaron needed to worry about was her getting in trouble because of him. He would have to put that aside for now, and work on what he could control because Mackenzie Ashton was something he definitely couldn't.

Aaron was close to the ninth level of his favorite computer game when the phone jolted him back to reality. He reluctantly paused his game and grabbed the receiver.

"What's up?"
"Hey, Aaron."
"Ryan, how are you?"
"I'm good. You sound like you are doing better."
"Yeah, I am. I gave it all to God and prayed about it and He actually answered me."
"What happened?"
"Well, I prayed about it and as soon as I got done and was on my way downstairs I heard a voice saying 'Ask and it will be given to you; seek and you will find; knock and the door will be opened to you. For everyone who asks receives; he who seeks finds; and to him who knocks, the door will be opened', I went into my mom's room where it was coming from and there was a preacher talking, and you know what their topic was?"
"What?"
"Seeking your Father! He was letting me know to go to my dad, and letting me know that he wanted me to find him. He answered my prayer! Isn't it incredible?"
"Aaron that is great, so did you talk to your mom or something? Are you going to go to his house?"
"Are you crazy? Of course I didn't tell my mom, I think she would have a heart attack. I'm going to go there myself when she is out of town."
"Slow down, Aaron, just listen to me for a minute, okay. I think you should pray about this some more. I don't think what you are going to do is what God intended."
"*What are you talking about*? Oh, so now you are God's interpreter? You know what He has to say?" Aaron was getting aggravated by his friends 'holier than thou attitude', who made him the expert anyway?
"That isn't what I said, Aaron. Just hear me out. It also doesn't take a genius to know a little about who God is. I know that God would never tell someone to disobey their parents, sneak around, and above all lie."

"Well, He told me to seek my father and the door would be opened to me, and I can't tell my mom so what does that leave me?"

"I don't know, but I do know that if I were you I would be praying about it more until I found out. Seriously, Aaron, I know that this is a mistake and you are going to end up getting in trouble."

"I think that you get your kicks off of pretending to be some Moses or something. Who do you think you are telling *me* what is right or wrong? I trusted you enough to tell you how God answered my prayer and you just squashed it! You are supposed to be my friend and all you're doing is bringing me down. I know what I heard earlier today so you can just shove all your hypocritical bull crap where the sun doesn't shine because I'm not going to listen anymore!" Aaron was screaming by the end of his tirade and slammed the phone down on its' receiver after his last sentence without waiting for a reply.

Aaron paced the circumference of his room trying to calm himself down. He was going through the conversation in his mind over and over again and instead of cooling off he was getting more angry. He walked to the full length mirror mounted on his bedroom door and slammed his fist into it shattering the glass and sending the frame crashing to the floor. Aaron stood stock still and took in deep breaths of air trying to calm the familiar rage from building anymore than it already had.

Aaron had learned six months ago not to hit at his walls anymore because after his mother had patched up the fourth hole he had punched through his bedroom wall she had had a serious talk with him about sending him to counseling. Aaron definitely did not want to go talk to some flaky therapist so he tried to take his anger out on his door which was much sturdier than the drywall. He looked down at his hand which was now covered in blood and was starting to sting.

"Dang it!" Aaron said aloud as he ran into the bathroom trying not to let it drip on the carpet. He washed all the glass out and discovered there were only a few deep cuts on his knuckles. As he was finishing wrapping up his wounded hand the telephone rang once again. He stalked back over to his phone, picked it up thinking it was Ryan, and angrily said, "What?!"

"Aaron, it's Mom, is every thing ok, what's wrong?" Aaron's mother asked concerned.

"Sorry, I thought you were someone else, I'm fine."

"Are you and Mackenzie in another fight? What happened?"

"No Mom, I just thought you were another telemarketer, they have been calling all day." Aaron was impressed with his quick recovery.

"Oh, I see. Well, I was calling because I'm on my way home from work. Do you want me to pick you up some soup or anything? How are you feeling?"

"Much better now, I think I just needed some extra sleep but maybe some of that soup from Kodiak Creek would help."

"Got it, I'll call and place the order now. I'll see you in about twenty minutes."

"Thanks Mom."

Aaron paced his room with his mood hanging over him like a dark rain cloud. He knows he has a tendency to fly off the handle under certain circumstances. He did feel guilty about the things he had said to Ryan. But he easily justified his reaction to what Ryan said because he's the one that doesn't have a father and in the end it's his decision on what to do about it. No one would ever be able to convince him otherwise. He wanted to believe that God wanted him to go to Florida because deep down Aaron knew that's what *he* wanted. He just needed an excuse to do it.

~8~

*'We all, like sheep, have gone astray,
each of us has turned to his own way;
and the Lord has laid on him the iniquity of us all.'
Isaiah 53:6 (NIV)*

Aaron conned his mother into thinking that the mirror had fallen by accident and his injury was a result of trying to clean it up. He didn't like lying to his mother but she had a tendency to over react. Aaron knew his anger sometimes got the best of him, but he definitely wasn't out of control like his mother would assume. Aaron listened as his mother and Ben discussed their plans for their trip the following week as he played solitaire at the table. He brain stormed on how he was going to be able to buy the tickets assuming that you had to be eighteen to purchase them. Aaron thought of Brandon, a second time senior that he met last year in a computer class. Aaron was sure he was eighteen by now. He figured Brandon would be his best shot at getting the tickets if he offered him something that would make it worthwhile.

After calling several of his friends he finally got Brandon's phone number. He quickly dialed as he shut his bedroom door. Instead of reaching the wayward senior Aaron spoke to his preoccupied and slightly agitated sister, who informed him that her brother went bowling tonight and then without further ado hung up on him. Aaron smiled as he hung up the phone and hoped that Brandon was headed to Sonny Lanes this evening.

The only dilemma now was convincing his mother, after missing a day of school that he was well enough to go out tonight. Aaron looked at his alarm clock and realized he better start working on his mom if he was going to meet Mackenzie at seven o'clock. He yelled out his bedroom door for his mom and crossed his fingers that she would let him go.

"Yeah hunny, what do you need? I'm kind of in the middle of something."
"Sorry to interrupt you, I just needed to ask you something."
"Sure, what's going on?"
"Well, I know I stayed home today and everything but I made a promise that I would go to the bowling alley tonight."
"Aaron you know the rules… no school, no play."
"I know but last week I made plans to meet with Mack and I didn't show and she just called to remind me about tonight and if I don't go I think she's going to think that I'm blowing her off or something."
Aaron knew he hit a soft spot by bringing up feminine emotions when his mom sat down on his bed and looked at him with concern. Aaron knows his mom's feelings for Mackenzie and he hated using that knowledge to get his way but he couldn't think of any other card to play.
"Why didn't you meet her last week?"
"I just forgot that's all."
"Well, Mack isn't one of your guy friends, Aaron. I know you two are good friends but you have to remember Aaron that she's a girl and girls interpret things, like forgetting, differently than you boys do."
"I know that's why I think it's important that I go, I mean I don't want her to think I don't want to hang out or anything."

Aaron's mom studied his face as she continued.

"Are you guys' *just* friends? You can tell me if there is more to it Aaron, your fifteen now and I like Mack a lot. I just want to know what's going on."

"Of course we are just friends, mom. That is it, I promise, and I know you really like her. I do too… as a friend."

Aaron's mom walked to the bedroom door and turned around as she was about to leave and smiled at her son.

"Well then, you better show up tonight so that she knows it. Just don't be too late, your curfew is eleven."

"Thanks mom."

Aaron left twenty minutes later and hurried the eleven blocks into town anxious to find out if Brandon would buy the tickets for him. He arrived at the brand new bowling alley a few minutes past seven and was surprised to see throngs of teenagers already flooding the entry way.

Aaron could smell the fresh paint as he made his way inside. He smiled at the cosmic theme the bowling alley was obviously trying to pull off with black walls and neon stars and planets hanging from the ceiling and painted on the walls. He looked around and saw Mack at lane 13 already changing her shoes.

Aaron made his way over to her after waiting in line for his shoes and sat down.

"Hey, thanks for getting the lane for us, what do I owe you?"

"I don't know, we find out when we are done. I guess you pay after at this place."

"There's a lot of people here, have you seen Brandon?"

"Brandon?" Mack quirked her brow not understanding what he was talking about.

"You know the senior Brandon that lives a couple blocks from you."

"Oh yeah, actually I did. Why?"

"I am going to see if he'll buy the ticket for me."

"Did I just hear you say ticket? You mean *tickets* right?"

Aaron didn't want to get into an argument with her, but he really didn't want her to get into trouble on his account. He was starting to lose hope that she was going to start seeing this his way.

"Listen Mack, I am really thankful for all you have done and I appreciate that you want to do this for me but I really don't think you should go, seriously just think about it."

"I have Aaron, and I am going with you so quit trying to change the inevitable. Can you do that for me?"

Aaron looked into her big green eyes and decided arguing was futile and smiled at her.

"So, I was saying I have to talk to Brandon about purchasing *tickets* for this trip me and a great friend of mine are taking in a little over a week."

He was rewarded with the most brilliant smile and jaunty attitude that only Mack can pull off and does whenever she wins an argument.

"Sounds more like it! I saw Brandon playing pool in the arcade when I got here. Find yourself a ball on your way back, I am ready to do some serious damage to your ego tonight."

Aaron raised his brows and grinned at that then turned to find Brandon. It didn't take long to locate him as he was the loudest one in the arcade. Aaron waited until Brandon was done throwing a slew of crude comments at one of his friends before interrupting. Brandon noticed Aaron and smiled.

"Hey Aaron, what's up?"

"Actually I needed to talk to you for a sec, do you have a minute?"

"Sure, what's up?" He responded as he walked towards Aaron. Brandon's friends reminded him to make it quick because they had money down on the game of pool they were playing.

"I wondered if you would do me a favor."

"That would depend on what it is."

"I need you to buy me a couple Greyhound tickets."
"What for?"
"It's a long story but I'll give you twenty bucks if you help me out."
"Twenty bucks....when do you need them by?"
"This week, will you do it?"
"Alright, I'll meet you Monday after school and we'll go get them but I want gas money too."
"Deal, thanks a lot man, I'll see you Monday by the stairs." Aaron turned and beamed ear to ear, his plans were taking form.

Aaron couldn't believe his luck that the only ball left that fit his hand was pink with big cheesy gold stars all over it and an even cheesier engraving by the finger holes that said 'Bowling Is Fun'. He was still grinning over his misfortune and wondering what sly remarks Mack was going to make at the sight of his very un-masculine ball when he reached their lane. Aaron froze mid-step as he heard a familiar jeering behind him.

"Hey look pintos and cheese made it!" Paul snickered.
Aaron could feel his pulse rise and his face flush. He turned ball in hand and glared at the three boys as he tried to calm himself down. He watched as Gus approached him with one hand curiously in his pocket.
"The kid should know by now just to stay home." Teddy bit out.
"I guess he hasn't figured it out yet." Gus icily remarked.
Aaron stood by the ball return frozen temporarily unable to trust himself or his rage as he watched Gus come within striking distance of him. He could hear the rustling of other teens starting to gather closer around them in hopes of seeing a fight, but he couldn't take his eyes off of Gus.
"Nice ball dork, it suits you."
"Back off Gus, I'm not in the mood for you right now." Aaron bit out between clenched teeth.

"In your dreams fairy," Gus returned as he shoved Aaron hard in the chest. Aaron tried to think of a way to calm the situation but was starting to not care. When Aaron just stared blankly at the larger boy it infuriated Gus. He pulled back his fist to punch Aaron and as he started to swing, Aaron was readying himself to deflect the blow by ducking, but instead of Gus's fist he saw a blur of red and immediately knew what had happened.

Aaron yelled from the depths of his soul as he looked down at the crumpled form of Mackenzie Ashton. He lost complete control at that moment as he looked up into the still jeering face of Gus and snapped. Aaron swung the hand that still held the bowling ball as hard as he possibly could and aimed for Gus's head. His arm was in mid-arch when it was suddenly stopped and pulled backwards. Aaron dropped the ball and struggled to get at the boy that had just hurt his best friend. A familiar voice from behind him started pulling him out of his rage. He saw Mack sit up and plead with her eyes for him to stop.

"Aaron don't do this," It was then Aaron realized the person holding him back from killing Gus was Ryan.

"Why don't you stay out of this punk?" Gus taunted as Ryan moved to stand beside Aaron, feeling confident that Aaron was under more control now.

"Do you feel like a real man now hitting a girl?" Ryan stared at the boy and Aaron watched in amazement as Gus started to cower before him even though he was bigger than Ryan and had his two friends there who were starting to back away.

As Aaron was helping Mack to her feet he watched the employees trying to make their way through the crowd.

"Alright everyone the excitements over now, let's go. You three, out of here now," the employees shouted while pointing at Gus, Paul, and Teddy.

"And we better not see you in here again!" With that they quickly turned to Mack, throwing questions a mile a minute at her.

"Are you ok? Do you want us to call the police and file a report? What can we do?"

"No, I'm really okay." When they didn't look like they believed her, she smiled and said, "Seriously, I'm okay, really." One of the employees handed her a bag of ice and she thanked him as she put it against her cheek.

"Mack what in the heck were you thinking? Do you think I can't take care of myself?!" Aaron was furious.

"No, I just wanted to help and if you yell at me one more time I'm gonna hit you myself!" Mack bit back matching him glare for glare. Ryan chose that precise moment to interrupt.

"Aaron, could I talk to you for a second please?"

"Who are you?" Mack looked at him speculatively.

"Ryan this is Mackenzie, Mack, Ryan Kinnley."

"Oh, he was the guy you hung out with last week, right?"

"Yeah, look Mack give me sec and keep that ice on your face." Without a backwards glance Aaron strode away from the two. Ryan gave Mack one of his lopsided grins, "It was nice to meet you," and hurried to catch up to Aaron.

"What was that all about?" Ryan's face showed his concern.

"You care?" Aaron looked bored and Ryan could sense his hostility.

"Of course I care, what's that suppose to mean?"

"Look, I don't need your help and I have taken care of that guy twice before without you so don't start thinking I need your help. I did just fine before I met you," he never once looked into Ryan's face as he was giving his speech.

"Aaron, no one said you needed a protector, I didn't interfere because I was scared for you. I interfered because I thought if you hit him with that ball you could have killed him." Ryan let his words soak into Aaron before he continued in the same steady calm voice. "I don't look at you and see a charity case....this may seem weird because I haven't known you very long, but when I look at you I see a little brother. And because I care what's going on with you I tend to say whatever I think without taking your feelings into consideration. I am sorry about earlier, I didn't mean to come across the way you took me, and I'm sorry your girlfriend got hurt over there."

"She's not my girlfriend alright. She's my *friend*, and I've known her since I was six. Forget about earlier…I know I can get pretty intense sometimes and I didn't mean to take it out on you. I know you were just telling me what you believe, but I guess you're right, there are some things I'm going to have to learn on my own." Aaron held out his hand to Ryan in a gesture of truce as he said "Friends?" Ryan looked at Aaron's outstretched hand, grabbed it and yanked Aaron into his embrace. The two smiled at each other. "I got to get back so I'll see you Sunday?"

"K, I'll see you there."

Aaron strolled to the seat next to Mackenzie and she excused herself from the three girls from school that were intent on playing nursemaid to her, and looked at Aaron without saying a word.

"I swear if you ever do anything that stupid again …."

"You'll what? Aaron I am not sitting here thinking that what happened was your fault, or mine. So don't you dare sit there and tell me that I'm not suppose to care if you are about to get jumped by three guys."

"Alright, let's just stop this okay. I just don't like seeing you get hurt, that's why I got so upset alright." Mack smiled at Aaron which completely confused him seeing he didn't think she was anywhere near the end of her emotional outburst.

Mack stood up walked towards the computer where she had already put in their names and turned to give him a challenging look, "You ready to get your butt kicked now?"

The two friends walked out of the bowling alley still razzing each other about their re-match that needed to take place because they had each won one game. Aaron and Mack walked in silence the last two blocks before they had to split in directions to go home. When they got to Miller Street and paused to say good bye, Mack was momentarily paralyzed as Aaron tilted her face up to his. Aaron started scrutinizing her swelled and slightly bruised cheek under the light of the street lamp. "You're sure your mom isn't going to be able to notice that, it's kind of obvious." Mack flushed at her foolish thoughts in misunderstanding his actions.

"It'll be fine," Mack promised as she walked to within inches of Aaron and slid her arms around his neck, holding onto him tightly she whispered against his neck, "thank you for taking care of me tonight, it's nice to know that I have a friend like you." Mack backed away from the embrace while looking into his eyes, then suddenly turned and started walking away from him towards her home.

Aaron was dumbstruck watching her leave. He didn't understand why he liked the hug so much from her. He has gotten hugged by her a thousand times before, why was now different? He watched her round the corner at the end of the block and started towards his house still reeling from his reaction to his best friend.

~9~

'Fathers, do not exasperate your children; instead, bring them up in the training and instruction of the Lord.'
Ephesians 6:4(NIV)

Aaron woke up to his mother yelling that the phone was for him. He groggily looked at his alarm clock realizing that it was eleven o'clock and smiled because Mack was already calling him. Aaron yelled "Got it mom!" as he grabbed his phone
"What's up brat?"
"I don't know about the brat part," replied a male voice.
"Ryan?"
"Hey, what's up?"
"Not much, just getting up actually, what's going on with you?"
"I was getting some friends together to play some ball at one o'clock and was wondering if you wanted to come."
"Yeah, I'll go."
"Pick you up at 12:30 then?"
"Alright, see you then."

As Aaron sat waiting for Ryan he picked up the cordless and dialed Mack's number.
"Hello?" A male voice slurred out.

"Is Mack there?"

"Who?!" the man practically yelled.

"Mack, is she there?"

"Oh, hang on." He could hear the man's voice scream Mackenzie's name at the top of his lungs several times.

When Mack picked up the phone Aaron said, "Hey, what was that all about?"

"Oh, I'm sorry, that was my dad. You just have to learn to ignore him."

"How's your cheek?"

"Oh it's fine, it's not swollen at all today, just a little bruised, it'll be fine."

"That's good to hear. I wanted to talk to you about yesterday."

"You're not going to yell at me again are you?"

"Of course not, I just wanted you to know how sorry I am that it even happened. It was my fault and it'll never happen again."

"What? Did you hit me, is that why it was your fault?" Mack asked sounding confuse.

"You're a girl and I was there and you still got hit."

Aaron was waiting for a response and was surprised to hear her laughter ringing through the phone.

"Thanks for squashing my ego." He blandly responded making her laugh even harder.

"I'm sorry, I'm sorry, I'm sorry." Mackenzie managed to chuckle out. "It's just funny how much I don't understand you sometimes, there's no logic there. But anyway I am glad you called, I wanted to ask if you would come over for dinner tomorrow night. My mom's making chicken parmesan and she's been asking me where you've been hiding, so it's time to make another appearance at my house."

"Sounds great, what time?"

"Around six?"

"Cool, so what are you doing today?"

"I am going to the mall with Sylvie, Andrea, and Vicky."

"While you're there get a Red Wings jersey."
"Why should I when I already have one."
"Yeah, but it's *my* Red Wings jersey."
"But it fits me sooo good."
Aaron heard her laughing as she hung up the phone.

Ryan arrived to pick up Aaron ten minutes early. Aaron hopped into the pick up truck ready for some fun. Ryan looked at Aaron apprehensively as he said, "I am not going to play today but I am going to go and watch. You can still play Jake and Billy and some other guys will be there."

Aaron looked at Ryan in confusion. "Why aren't you going to play?"

"I'm not feeling so good, so I am just going to watch."

"You just called an hour ago… If you are sick you should go home and go to bed or something."

"You don't understand. I have leukemia and I get sick sometimes, I really try not to change my plans if I can help it. The chemo therapy is what makes me a bit weak and so I'll just sit this one out. I really wanted to talk to you about this before, but I didn't get a chance." Aaron's chin hit the floor. His mouth hung open as he tried to comprehend all that was said.

"I thought if you believed in God, He wouldn't let this kind of stuff happen. I mean seriously almost your entire life is devoted to church or some form of it. I don't know any other kid that has a faith like you do. Why? I don't get it." Aaron was shook to the very core of his being that he could lose someone he cared for and almost as shook in the realization that he cared as much as he did.

"I believe everything happens for a reason and I have faith that everything will work out as God has planned it. It's really not all that bad and I will overcome, I have faith in that." Aaron was astonished at his friend's attitude and truly admired his courage.

****

Mack called Aaron at 5:00 to remind him that he was supposed to be at her house in an hour. Aaron assured her that he would be there and smiled as he hung up the phone thinking of how Mack always tries to mother him. He shook his head as he got up to go find his mother to tell her that he wouldn't be home for dinner because he had forgotten he was supposed to be at Mack's.

Aaron arrived to Mack's house at 5:45 and knocked on the door. He smiled at Mrs. Ashton when she opened the door for him and thanked her for inviting him over for dinner. The five foot, one inch tall robust woman with flaming red hair and freckles smiled up at him and gave him a hug as she called for Mack to come down stairs.

"You are very welcome, Aaron. It has been so long since I've seen you, what's kept you so busy lately?"

"School mostly, what about you?" The banter with Mrs. Ashton always came easy for him. She always seemed happy and interested.

"Work as always, let me get this dinner out and we can talk at the table, it should be ready soon. Go ahead and make yourself comfortable," she grinned as she made her way back to the kitchen.

Aaron smelled the aroma that filled the house and his mouth started watering, he tried to remember whether or not he had eaten lunch. He glanced up the stairs and wondered what was keeping Mack then walked over to the pictures lining the base of the stairs and grinned at the little red headed girl with large green eyes staring back at him with cut off shorts and skinned up knees. He filed the image of the chicken legged girl so he could razz her about it later.

"What are you doing?" Mack inquired from the top step.

"Checking out the younger Mackenzie," he couldn't help but smile wide at her and she surmised he thought she was an ugly child.

"Well, I've seen a few of you in the tub so don't be getting too smart with me, I know where your mom keeps them and I know the kids on the school paper too." Mackenzie Ashton was confident as she strolled down the stairs and gave him a toothy smile. Aaron laughed and decided to change the subject from him being publicly humiliated to a more pleasant one.

"Where's little man?"

"Monster Max? He's in the basement playing video games, he'll be up in a few. Are you hungry?"

"Starved, let's go see if your mom needs any help."

"No wonder she likes you so much no one else would think to offer."

"I like your mom," with that they went into the kitchen to see that she was already placing the food onto the plates.

They sat down at the table as Mrs. Ashton called for Max. The red headed boy bolted into the kitchen at top speed and almost slid into the cupboards.

"Aaron! When did you get here?"

"Just a few minutes ago, how have you been?"

"Great! I just got my guy to level fifty-four!"

"Cool buddy!" Aaron rubbed the six year olds head as he took the seat to the right of Aaron.

Mrs. Ashton sat just as the front door slammed and the entire table went silent. Aaron's fork was half way to his mouth when he realized the entire table had gone deadly still. He looked at Mack and realized her face had lost all its color.

"Jackie!" A man's voice boomed through the small colonial, he sounded angry.

"Let's go Aaron." Mack's voice was trembling as she grabbed his hand and stood up from the table. Aaron was troubled at the way she was acting, she looked terrified.

"Now?" Aaron immediately wished he could take back his words at the look of pleading he saw in her eyes as she tugged on his hand to get up. He stood just as a large six foot tall dark haired man with a beard walked into the kitchen. Aaron recognized Mr. Ashton although he had only met him in passing a few times before.

"I thought you weren't going to be home till ten or eleven tonight, George, let me get you a plate." Mrs. Ashton scurried through the kitchen hastily making his dish while Mack continued pulling Aaron out of the room. Mr. Ashton was swaying as he stood glaring at Aaron through glossy eyes.

"Just keep going please," Mack whispered so only Aaron could hear her.

"Where do you think you are going missy?!" Mr. Ashton bellowed even though they were standing just feet away. "We're having dinner you need to sit your fanny down, and send your friend home," he continued to slur.

"I'm sorry mom," she said softly as she grabbed Aaron's hand and started to run, pulling him in her wake. The front door slammed behind them as they heard Mr. Ashton's irate roar and feet stumbling behind them.

Aaron ran with her still holding her hand, when they were six blocks away and still running he looked down at her and saw the tears streaming without abandon down her pale face. He did what any true friend would do and kept running with her.

~10~

'Where can I go from your Spirit? Where can I flee from your presence? If I go up to the heavens, You are there; if I make my bed in the depths, You are there. If I rise on the wings of the dawn, if I settle on the far side of the sea, even there your hand will guide me, your right hand will hold me fast.
Psalm 139:7-10(NIV)

Aaron was out of breath by the time Mackenzie stopped running ten blocks from her house. He was panting when she dropped his hand that she was still holding and went to her knees with her back to him under the street lamp. Mack continued to sob uncontrollably, her long fire red hair shielding her face from his vision.

Aaron now understood so many things about her, why she always put on a tough guy facade, why she brings her brother with her almost everywhere she goes, why he has only met her father twice and those times it was when he unexpectedly dropped by, and why she is at his house and he rarely goes to hers. Aaron's next realization choked the breath out of him as he came to his knees beside her. He now understood why she has always put up with his angry explosions at her or whoever, she was used to it.

Mack sat rocking with her arms hugging her knees to her chest. He couldn't bare to watch her, but was unsure what to say or how to comfort her. Aaron moved behind her and put his arms around her own and said nothing because he felt the familiar fury starting to build deep within him. He was starting to tremble with the anger that some man that was supposed to love her and protect her was most likely hurting her in every possible way. He wanted to shelter her, he wanted her to be happy, and if he was the only person who would, well then by God, he would. Aaron then did the only thing left to do – he prayed.

Mack's head came up as her breathing calmed and she whispered out, "I'm so sorry you had to see that. I didn't want you or anyone to know. I thought he wasn't going to be home tonight." Mack was trembling as she looked up to meet his eyes. Aaron was still holding her, his face inches from hers, the soft light from the lamp casting a glow around the two.

"I don't understand why you are apologizing Mackenzie, I am the one who is sorry. You never have to keep anything from me… Is he hurting you?" Aaron looked into her clear moss green eyes and knew that she would tell him the truth.

"He has hurt all of us, my mom, brother, and me. I have gotten better at knowing when to leave and when to just stay in a different room than him. There are times he is sober and he is actually funny, but more and more lately he has been drinking and I just have to watch out for my brother and me when he is. He wasn't going to hurt anyone tonight but I ran with you because I was embarrassed of what he would say, he can get extremely loud and mean with his words," she explained trying to pull herself together.

His nearness was starting to make her more emotional so she pulled out of his embrace and sat on the sidewalk facing him. He sat across from her looking into her eyes and gave her a moment before asking her more. "How has he hurt you?" He asked trying to keep his own rage in check and not let it show in his voice.

She looked down at her hands as she started to speak and never looked up. "He has slapped me…there was one time when I was twelve that I had left the garage door open and he pushed me and I fell down the stairs but he didn't mean to, he didn't realize I was so close to the stairs when he pushed me, and remember about seven months ago when you were over and asked me where the porcelain music box was that you had gotten me? Well, it was shattered by my dad when I didn't get my bed made to his liking. I still have it, but it doesn't play music anymore." She looked up for a moment to see him nod and then focused on her hands again. She finished her recounting shaking and trying her best not to cry, crying never helped anyone.

Mack looked up at him hoping not to see revulsion in his eyes. Aaron watched her meet his gaze as a single tear slipped from his eye. He opened up his arms and she crawled into his embrace as the two friends tried to give comfort to the other. Aaron had no idea how long they had been sitting on the sidewalk holding onto each other when she spoke again.

"Don't hate my mom or dad or anything, promise me."

"Mackenzie, I don't know what your mom is thinking by letting you and your brother get hurt like that, but I don't hate her. Your dad needs help, I don't hate him, but you need to tell someone about this Mackenzie, it's not right." Aaron was surprised he could actually say he didn't hate her dad without puking.

"You can't tell anyone, you don't understand Aaron, my mom can't do it by herself. You have to promise me you won't say a word to anyone." Mack was pleading with her eyes trying to make him understand.

Aaron could sense the urgency in her plea and decided to wait to press her further on telling someone, she had been through enough tonight. "I won't tell unless you tell me its okay," he grabbed her hand and squeezed for emphasis, "I promise." She nodded, fully trusting in his promise.

"You have to promise me something though. If your dad even smells like he has been drinking, get you and Maxwell out of there.... I don't want you taking any chances at all with you or him, you promise?"

"I promise."

Aaron stood and helped Mack to her feet. He kissed her forehead, grabbed her hand and together they started walking back. They arrived in her driveway and he turned her towards him. "Are you going to be okay in there?"

"Yes, of course I'll be fine." Aaron could sense that she was nervous by the way she was wringing her hands and how she didn't look him in the eye when she said it.

"Mack, don't go back if you think something's going to happen to you." As the words came out of his mouth there was a huge crash and yelling coming from within Mackenzie's house. He looked up at the house and then back at Mackenzie.

"You aren't going back in there, what about Max?"

"He got picked up at 6:30 by his friend from school for a birthday party, I will get into so much trouble if I don't go home, I have to go back."

"And then what? Have him throw *you* into a wall like he is doing to your house plants?"

"You just don't understand, I know how to calm him down. He won't hurt me," she tried to convince him, maybe even herself too.

"Do you actually hear yourself?" He didn't expect an answer as he stared at her. "You aren't going back in that house tonight, and that's that."

"Where am I supposed to go?" She met his stare as both friends lost their energy to fight.

"You are coming with me." Aaron grabbed her hand and hauled her in his wake towards his house. Mack ran to keep up with him and when they arrived at Aaron's house she shook her head at him.

"No Aaron, I can't stay here. Your mom will flip, you know I can't." Mack was starting to back away from him as he yanked her back and started walking up the steps onto his porch.

"She'll never know you are here, she leaves early tomorrow for some class reunion for Ben in Flint and we'll have the house to ourselves. I want you to stay until things cool down at your house, don't shake your head at me girl. That's it, you are staying." With that Aaron pulled Mack through the front door of his house into the dark entry way and quietly shut the door behind them.

~11~

'For God so loved the world that He gave His one and only Son, that whoever believes in Him shall not perish but have eternal life. For God did not send His son into the world to condemn the world, but to save the world through Him.'
John 3:16-17(NIV)

Mack tugged on his arm and tried to lip sink to him "no" so as not to make noise, but he paid her no attention as he continued to maneuver through the house and up the stairs towards his room. She couldn't believe what she was doing when they finally reached his bedroom and he shoved her inside and flipped on the light. "I think you have seriously lost your mind," Mack whispered with a disgruntled look on her face as she jerked her hand free.

"I have? You know what? …I'm not even going to go there with you."

"What? Go ahead and say it," she challenged with a new determination in her eye.

"I'm not the one getting pushed around and pretending nothing is wrong," he was stunned when she stood up, walked over to him, squared her shoulders, and slapped him across the face. She stood in front of him staring him down waiting for him to lash back at her.

It took him a few minutes to recover, but when he did he was ashamed of judging her and he realized he deserved a lot more than a slap. It wasn't his place to judge her actions when he has never been in her shoes. "Can you forgive me? That was so wrong of me."

She looked surprised at his response and staring at his downcast face looking somewhat uncomfortable it was all she could do not to laugh. She couldn't help herself. He looked at her face to see if she was going to slap him again and when he saw the mirth in her eyes and her lips trying hard not to give in to her obvious amusement, he was surprised but started smiling back. "You forgive me then?"

"Yes, you brat." She laughed and slugged him in the chest. "Do you realize that if my parents knew I was here I would be sent to a boarding school? Seriously, have you thought about what people will think if they catch us?"

"What are we doing that's so bad?"

"Nothing."

"Well then, don't you think it's about time we stop caring so much about what people think?"

"I agree, but when those people are our parents, I care."

"No one's going to know so quit worrying."

Aaron told her he would be back in a minute and quietly snuck into the hallway. He returned a few minutes later with two extra pillows and a blanket.

"You take the bed and I'll sleep on the floor, do you need a drink or something?"

"No, you sleep in your own bed." She tried to grab the pillows from him but he held fast and just eyed her to quit.

"Look, I am the one who dragged you here. The least I can do is let you sleep in the bed, now go lay down." She watched him arrange the blanket on the floor and flip the switch to the light as she sat dumbly on the edge of his twin bed. She listened to the sound of him getting situated on the floor and decided that she was tired and laid down on his bed deciding she would sleep on top of the blankets. She curled on her side listening to his breathing and staring through the dim light towards the far wall. After some time had passed and she assumed he was already fast asleep she whispered into the darkness, "Thank you."

Aaron smiled into the night.

****

Morning light shone through the curtains casting shadows into the room as Mack stretched and then bolted upright as comprehension of where she was struck her. She stared nervously around the room and realized Aaron wasn't there. What was she suppose to do now? What if his mom hadn't left after all and he's downstairs explaining to her right now why there is a girl in his bed.

She heard footsteps coming towards the bedroom and flew off the bed and searched for a place to hide. She ran towards the closet and was nearly inside when the door slowly opened. Aaron peeked in then threw the door open wide when he realized Mack wasn't in bed anymore, he saw her flushed cheeks and quirked a brow at her. "What are you doing?"

Relief poured through her as she stared into his amused face. He had showered, his hair was still damp, and he had on fresh clothes.

"I thought you were your mom. Is she gone?"

"Yeah, and how the heck are you going to come to Pensacola with me if you're going to be this jumpy? You do realize we're going to be gone for at least four days right?"

She smiled at his quip, "I'll be just fine when I don't have to worry about parents." She watched him get his shoes out of the closet. "Where are you going at 8:15 in the morning?"

"I just have somewhere to be, there's a brand new toothbrush in the bathroom, are you going to hang out for a while? I'll be back around eleven." He asked without looking at her.

"Where are you going?" she asked again thinking that he was trying to hide something from her.

"Just got something to take care of, I won't be long." He knew he wasn't going to be able to get out the door without having to lie to her and he just couldn't make himself do it.

"So, you don't want to tell me? I thought we weren't keeping any more secrets." She put her hands on her hips and waited for him to respond.

He deliberately stalled by finishing putting on his shoes and then stood up and faced her. "I'm going to church. It starts at nine and should be over by 10:30, thus I will be back by eleven, anything else?"

Her brows knit together, "Church?"

"Yes, church, I started going last week. That's where I met Ryan."

"Why didn't you tell me?"

"I didn't even know how I felt about it, but I like going and now I know all that God stuff is real. I can't explain it, but it is. So, are you going to be here when I get back?" He was uncomfortable talking to her about it and kept expecting her to call him a freak or something.

"No, I'm going to come with you if you can give me five minutes to freshen up." She started out of his room.

"Seriously?"

"Well, if you believe it's real then it's worth checking out," she smiled at him and walked to the bathroom.

They entered the church and made their way through the cluster of people crowding the entry way towards the sanctuary. Aaron noticed Pastor John by the open set of double doors greeting people as they entered and smiled as he approached him.

The young pastor enveloped Aaron in an embrace. "It's great to see you again, how are you?"

"Great, this is my friend Mackenzie, Mack this is Pastor John, the youth pastor." Pastor John shook her hand with both of his and gave her a genuine smile as he welcomed her to the service.

When they started into the enormous sanctuary Mack whispered, "Are people here always this chipper?" She was squeezing herself closer to his side and he could tell she was uncomfortable.

Aaron spotted Ryan talking to Jake and Billy in the third row on the right of the sanctuary. He pointed them out to Mack as they walked towards them. Ryan noticed them and waved as he made room for two more. "Are you feeling okay?" Aaron inquired.

Ryan flashed a grin and patted Aaron on the shoulder before turning his attention to Mackenzie. "Mack, right?" Ryan gave Mack a lopsided smile as he shook her hand.

"Ryan, right?" She smiled back, although inside she was gritting her teeth at the way she imagined he must look at her. She never went to church and didn't do volunteer work with her spare time. She figured he just hid his true feelings about her well and for Aaron for that matter.

"I'm glad you came."

"Me too," she said to her shoes.

"Mack, this is Jake and Billy." He gestured to the two standing next to him as they smiled at her. "Aaron, good to see you."

As the music finished the pastor made his way to the podium. He started relating a story about an experience he had. He told of the amazing sacrifice Jesus made on the cross but was confused on why God would do it.

"Self sacrifice is easier than the sacrifice of a loved one. Being a father myself I know that I wouldn't have been able to make such a sacrifice and asked God in prayer why He could sacrifice His only Son for the world." He made a poignant point when you think about how messed up the world really is. "He still made that sacrifice even though so many people reject Him, and God answered him. He said, '*I didn't do it for the world, I did it for you.*' God made me understand that when we look at the world we see it as a whole. When God looks at the world He sees individuals, He sees each and every one of us.

So when Jesus was going through the most horrific torment anyone can imagine and God His Father was watching His Son die, He thought of you, and He did it all because He wanted you to understand how much He loves you." The pastor continued on.

Aaron looked over at Mack and saw her wipe a tear away with the back of her hand, and he was so happy she felt the truth in the pastor's words the same way he did.

After the service was over Jake pulled Aaron off to the side inquiring about a basketball game they were planning for this Thursday. Aaron was setting up a ride with Jake when he realized he had left Mack alone. He looked over his shoulder to see her standing a few feet away from him laughing at something Billy was saying as he gestured with his hands. Aaron tensed and his teeth clenched, he couldn't understand why he was reacting the way he was at seeing them talk but he definitely didn't like it. He finished speaking to Jake and turned to go over to Mack and Billy trying to calm his nerves. 'I must not have gotten enough sleep last night,' Aaron thought to himself. It was the only reason he could come up with for why he was acting so moody.

~12~

'...Holy, holy, holy is the Lord God Almighty, who was, and is, and is to come.'
Revalation4:8(NIV)

    Mack stood in front of the church staring out into the mass of cars trying to leave after the service. She breathed in the warm morning air and let the sun shine on her face. She sensed someone behind her and turned to see Aaron there. "I have to get home now."
    "Is everything going to be ok?"
    "Yeah, I'll get in trouble, but it shouldn't be too bad. My mom understands, it's not as bad as you think."
    "Well, from what I know about your dad so far, I know that when he looks at you he doesn't see what I see. Because if he did he wouldn't do the things he does. So as far as I am concerned, he's a bum and he doesn't deserve a kid like you." He watched as her face tried to hide unshed tears as she remembered using the same words to comfort Aaron about his own father.
    "Thanks Aaron, I'll call you later." She turned and walked away while Aaron watched her leave from the steps of the church.

    Ryan caught up to Aaron in the parking lot. "Hey, I was going to get something to eat and see what's playing at the show, you want to come?" Aaron hopped into Ryan's car and within minutes was laughing at one of his stories. They decided to stop at a Coney Island and were halfway through their second Coney dog when Aaron suddenly asked "When did you know God was real?"

"Actually, I was in a juvenile detention facility."

"You mean like a jail for kids?"

"Yeah, I got caught stealing my third car and I was already on probation for setting the woods behind my house on fire."

"Wait a minute, you're seventeen right, when did all this happen?"

"I was thirteen at the time." Aaron tried to keep his astonishment in check as he stared with new eyes at this boy that he thought was every mother's dream child. "My parents hadn't visited me at juvi in over a week and I thought that they had given up on me. I already had the possibility of staying in the facility until my eighteenth birthday."

"What happened?"

"For the first time in my life I prayed. I prayed that if God would help my parents to forgive me and get me home then I would do anything He wanted. A few days later at my court hearing everything changed. My mother started crying when she saw me and hugged me as if I had been gone a year. My dad pleaded with the judge and he promised that he would do whatever he had to do to get me off the drugs I was on and get my life straight again. I've never been in trouble with law since that day and I've never stopped thanking the Lord either."

"Did you ever find out what God wanted you to do in return?"

"I always knew what He had wanted in return…me."

At seven o'clock Aaron got home and was hurrying through his homework when the phone rang. He picked the phone up on the second ring and was surprised to hear Mack on the other end.

"Haven't lost your phone privileges I see?"

"Worse, my computers are gone for a whole month."

"Did you tell them where you were?"

"I told them I slept in Sylvie's camper in front of her house, I think they bought it. I wanted to tell you thanks for last night. I was just embarrassed and I didn't want you to see that side of my family."

"You know you don't have to worry about that with me. You are my bud, none of that stuff matters, you know that… right?"

"I know, well thanks anyway. I have to go though, my mom has me doing manual labor today and I'm supposed to be cleaning the garage right now. So, I'll see you tomorrow. You are getting the tickets with Brandon after school right?"

"That's the plan. I'll see you at school."

****

Aaron stepped through the front doors after school with a feeling of exhilaration and scanned the meandering students for Brandon's face. He wasn't there. "I just knew it," Aaron thought to himself. "What am I going to do now?" Aaron thought about calling Ryan and asking him for a ride to the bus station, but had a sinking feeling he wouldn't do it since he thought he was crazy for going in the first place.

The overcast day was the perfect representation of the mood he was quickly developing. He sat on the steps hoping that Brandon had just gotten held up by a teacher.

"Hey dude, what's up?" Aaron heard his friend's voice before he saw him.

"How have you been, Justin?" Aaron smiled at his friend who took a seat on the stairs next to him.

"Not to bad, so you are ditching me next week, but you want me to cover for you?" Justin looked at Aaron like he wasn't quite sure if he should be mad at him or not.

"I am not trying to ditch you. The reason I'm not going to be able to stay is because I am going to find my real dad, he lives in Florida. I have never met him and it's very important to me. I would really appreciate it if you could help me out."

"I just figured you were going to hang out with Ralph or something. I didn't know it was all that. You can count on me. I got your back in this one." His dark haired friend with hazel eyes stood and threw his backpack over his shoulder. "I hope you find him." He smiled and started down the steps.

"Thanks man, I really appreciate it." Aaron called after Justin. Aaron heard honking and turned to see Brandon in his gray 1980 Oldsmobile Cutlass Brougham four door with big rust spots all over it pulling up to the front of the school.

Three hours later Aaron was talking to his mom in the kitchen as she was washing the dishes recounting for the fifth time what was happening next week while she was out of town.

"So how much money do you think you will need? You only have school two of the days we are gone and you will need some spending money. Do you have any idea what you boys are going to be doing?" The phone rang and Aaron leapt at the opportunity to get out of the conversation with his mother. He ran up the stairs taking them two at a time with the cordless from the kitchen.

"So how did it go? Did you get the tickets?" There was so much excitement in Mack's voice, Aaron couldn't help but smile.

"Yes, I got the tickets. It worked without a problem. They didn't ask us for anything, we just bought them. We got one ticket for free with that companion deal they have, so it is all set."

"How much was it?"

"It was $169.00 for both tickets, so I have about $255.00 left, but I think my mom is giving me money for spending and food for the week. I think that'll be enough." Aaron was in high spirits. For the first time in his life he was taking control and it felt great. He was still nervous about meeting his dad but he felt better that he was finally doing something about it. What father wouldn't want to meet his own kid, right?

"Well, I have about $140.00 and my mom is giving me some cash too for going to Sylvie's."

"How are you going to get around the fact that they might call Sylvie's house?"

"I am going to have my mom's cell phone next week so she can get a hold of me. If she calls I will just answer and say I'm out with Sylvie somewhere. So when do we leave?"

"Sunday at three, but we have to be there at two, that's what they said."

"Great, I got it all worked out on this end, how about you?"

"I have it covered. I'll talk to you more about it tomorrow."

Aaron prayed before he went to sleep that God would be with him and Mack on their trip to find his father.

****

Tuesday's history test went better than Aaron expected, he was sure of most of the answers and was in high spirits because he really needed the good mark. He saw Mack after fifth period wearing his Red Wings jersey and flares, her hair free down her back and a wide grin on her face.

"You look like you're in a good mood, what's up?"

"I think I may have just pulled my history grade up to the C range, what's going on with you?"

"Nothing, but I'm as board as spit at home computerless, let's hang out tonight."

"Actually, I have plans with Ryan. I thought you had hockey tonight?"

"No, the coach has got strep or something. Can I come, or are you guys doing some male bonding?" She smiled as she joked with him freely. "You're probably going to scope out chicks or something." There was laughter in her eyes and Aaron decided not to keep it from her anymore.

"No, actually we were going to church tonight."

"On a Tuesday? Are you serious?" She was smiling expecting a quick come back.

"Yes, I'm serious I went last week, it was good."

"You really *are* going to church?"

"Ryan's picking me up at 6:30. Do you want to ride with us?"

"I guess so. I'll be over around six." She forced a smile. Aaron could tell she was uncomfortable with the whole church thing. She was willing to go though, so that was a start he guessed. He didn't like feeling that she was somehow missing out on something that she didn't even realize was there, but she was.

When Mackenzie arrived on Aaron's porch a few minutes after six she could hear laughing coming from inside. She was about to knock on the door when a figure to her right caught her eye. She swung around and gasped before she realized it was Aaron. "You scared me half to death, what are you doing out here?"

"Waiting for you, did you eat yet, my mom still has dinner out if you want some."

"I ate, thanks. Your family seems to be having fun in there, so why are you out here? I'm not stupid enough to think you couldn't wait to see me."

"They just get on my nerves sometimes. Married people shouldn't be so flirty and when they are I just really want to hit Ben, so I came out here. Can we change the topic?"

"Absolutely… so what's this Tuesday night thing all about? Is Sunday not enough for you?"

"Tuesday is the youth group, and last week it was really good."

"The church thing is great and all, but I don't know if I believe in the whole 'there is something bigger than me out there'. I mean what's the use in believing in something that you can't see?"

"I know exactly what you mean because I thought that way too. I just want you to know that there is a lot more out there than you think.

Find the truth out for yourself. You are the only one who can decide what you will believe in or not. But you should find out, because after all, what if you are wrong?"

~13~

'Now faith is being sure of what we hope for and certain of what we do not see.'
Hebrews 11:1 (NIV)

As the Tuesday night youth group service came to a close Mackenzie Ashton took a deep breathe as she tried to take in all that she had just heard. She looked around at the many faces, some she recognized from school and many she didn't as they started to file out of the large sanctuary. She looked up at the high beamed room with its warmly painted walls in maroons and huge painted hangings of mountains and streams. She wondered why she felt so different when she came here. She noticed last time she had come that she was inordinately calmer when she had sat down and started to *really* listen. But now it was almost palpable, this peace she felt inside. Like nothing else that had ever happened or ever would happen really mattered when she was here.

Ryan tapped Mackenzie on her shoulder and pulled her from her reverie. "We were thinking of going to grab a bite to eat, do you want to come? Otherwise I can take you home." She stared into his warm brown eyes as he smiled down at her. She felt no condescension from him. She started to wonder why she had assumed that's what she would see. Maybe she had been so apprehensive about him because she figured he thought she wasn't a good person because she didn't believe the same things that he did. She was after all a big old sinner in his eyes because of his beliefs, or so she thought. She wasn't completely ignorant of the different religions and what some people believed in. Mackenzie realized at that moment that it was she that was stereotyping and being irrational, not him. She swallowed hard the truth that her eyes now were opened to, and replied, "Sure, I'd love to go."

Aaron, Ryan, Mackenzie, Jake, and Billy pulled into the parking lot of Kodiak Creek, a fantastic restaurant that always made you feel as if you were at a lodge up north when you were there. It was a very cozy place and even more importantly, the food was always excellent. The five teens ordered their sandwiches and drinks and started talking while they waited for their food to come.

Aaron was still thinking about the service while the others chatted about the latest movie that Jake and Billy had just seen. Aaron interrupted them, "Something that Pastor John had said tonight has really been making me think. When he said that if you have faith as small as a mustard seed you could tell a mountain to move from here to there and it will move. I don't really understand what he was saying by that."

Jake answered him, "I think what that scripture means is that even if you only have a small amount of faith, anything is possible. That if you believe in God, absolutely nothing, even moving a mountain, is impossible if it is His will. Their food arrived at the table as Billy and Ryan agreed.

"That seems so awesome, it is almost unreal to me," Aaron replied.

"God did part the sea for the Israelites to escape, saved Jonah from the belly of a whale, not to mention raising Lazarus from the dead. What's so impossible about moving a mountain?" Ryan asked, a small grin coming across his expressive face. He was making Aaron think.

Think like he never had before about the awesomeness of God and the power He had in Aaron's life, if he would let Him, and Ryan knew it.

Mack sat too engrossed in the conversation to eat as Jake and Billy scarfed down the Monte Cristos they had ordered. "I am not completely ignorant of bible stories Ryan, *Jesus* raised the dead guy, and *Moses* was the guy God used to part the sea. I haven't heard of any seas parting lately, and there definitely hasn't been anyone like Moses around in quite a while. *Miracles* just don't happen anymore." Aaron finished and picked up his turkey club.

"Actually, miracles happen every day in peoples' lives. They just don't make the six o'clock news. Premature children are born every day with no chance of survival that do, barren mothers are having children, and people with terminal diseases are being healed with no explanation science can come up with. Everyone's 'sea parting' is different Aaron." Ryan explained as he ate.

Mack sat uncomfortably contemplating whether or not to ask the question she had wanted to ask since they had started talking. She listened intently as they shared their thoughts and wanted to believe in what they were saying, who wouldn't want to believe in something that was so strong and loved you more than anyone and had the power to help you no matter what the circumstance, and wanted to. She decided she would take the chance of them looking at her like she was an imbecile. She couldn't help it, she wanted to know if there was an explanation to what she sees. "I don't understand how there can be an all powerful and all loving God that sees everything that happens here on earth and doesn't intervene. If He loves us so much why do children die of starvation every day? Why is there so much disease and destruction? Why would He let so many die in wars that are in His name? I can't believe that there is a God out there that would let this world be what it is." Mack choked out her last sentence as a tear streaked down her cheek.

Ryan looked at her and leaned over the table and took hold of her hand to comfort her. "I believe God wants us to love Him above all, and to *really* love someone there has to be a choice of something else. If there was only good and no evil we wouldn't have the choice, and without choice there isn't real love."

"I don't understand why He doesn't just come here and take all the pain away and make everyone understand."

"If He was to appear today and take all the evil away from this world and make everyone obey Him like He wants us to, how could we really love Him? We would *have* to, and love isn't something you can force someone to feel. He uses the bad stuff for His purpose in helping us to grow. God doesn't cause the bad things to happen, people do. I want to tell you something that God helped me to understand not too long ago. The pain we feel here on earth is just a moment in time compared to eternity. A child starving to death is an unbelievable tragedy, but to that same child in heaven it will seem like a distant memory or a faded moment of long ago."

Mack nodded new understanding to Ryan as she crumpled inside. She knew he was speaking truth to her, she could feel it deep in her soul.

~14~

'But the Counselor, the Holy Spirit, whom the Father will send in My name, will teach you all things and will remind you of everything I have said to you.'
John 14:26 (NIV)

Saturday morning Aaron was awakened by his mother's prodding at six in the morning. "We've got to go to the airport now hunny. The money for you for the week is on the counter downstairs. When you get up get your stuff together and head over to Justin's. I love you, and I'll call you on the cell phone when we get to the hotel to give you the number where we are, okay?"

"Alright mom, have a good time. I'll talk to you later." Aaron hugged his mother and kissed her dutifully on the cheek, then waved to Ben who was hovering at the doorway to his room.

"Take care Aaron, we'll talk to you soon," Ben said as he pulled at his wife's jacket to get her moving out of Aaron's room, anxious to get going.

"Okay Ben, have a safe trip." With that they were gone. Aaron heard the front door close, then the garage door open and shut as he fell back to sleep.

Aaron prayed diligently as was routine that their trip on the morrow would go smoothly and that God would be with and watch over them as they made their way across the country. Aaron called Justin around eleven in the morning to see if he could stay there tonight so he could at least hang out with him for one night. Justin anxiously agreed to have Aaron over and started eagerly planning the evening. "Yeah we could go to the bowling alley tonight, or if that is lame we could go to the movies or something, that new Tom Hanks' movie looked cool. Or we could go to the mall and hang out. My mom will give us a ride just about anywhere."

"Sounds good, I'll be over there within an hour, I'm just finishing packing." They hung up and Aaron grinned at his good fortune with the friends he has. Aaron finished packing and called Mack before he left to let her know his plans. They decided to meet at church the following morning and then they would attack a plan to get a ride to the bus station by two o' clock.

Aaron and his exuberant friend decided on playing paintball at a local indoor arena. Justin was a paintball fanatic and owned three paintball guns and had cases of paintballs in his garage. Aaron really didn't want to spend that much money but Justin argued that he wouldn't have to buy the paintballs or rent a gun which would make it half the cost it normally should have been to go. Aaron had to borrow clothes from Justin because he didn't bring any that could get trashed by paintballs. Justin gave him a black pair of sweats and a dark sweatshirt to put on over his jeans and t-shirt. Aaron looked like a cat burglar, but decided his get up was better than what Justin had put on. He looked like he had jumped out of a G.I. Joe action figure box wearing all camouflage with three utility belts for extra ammo around his waist and slung over his shoulder. He even had the boots to match. Aaron teased Justin mercilessly on the way there, but Justin just shrugged and smiled.

It was worth the thirty dollars Aaron decided after an hour of playing. The paintball arena was an old warehouse that was perfect for the game. It had five levels that included a run down mock gas station, cat walks, old decrepit cars and trucks, and even a basement with every kind of cubby and nook you can imagine to hide away in.

He was wedged between a wall and a nasty couch on the floor of a pretend living room when he heard an opponent coming down the stairs to his right. Aaron signaled to his partner, a ten year old kid named Nick, who then moved into position away from the dilapidated fridge he had been using for cover to be able to get a better shot at the figure trying to move soundlessly down the stairs. Aaron got up on his haunches and readied himself to fire as soon as the culprit made it to the bottom. In the somewhat dim light the figure came to the bottom and Aaron and Nick unloaded on the ignorant person who completely walked into their base without thinking there would be defenders protecting their flag. When the figure started screaming and waving his arms Aaron couldn't help but crack up as he realized he and his young partner had just shot the referee with about ten paintballs. Nick started spewing out apologies as Aaron laughed so hard his cheeks hurt.

Aaron was surprised at how much fun he actually had had. He was filthy, had welts all over and had laughed so hard his stomach still hurt. On the way back to Justin's house he was thinking about buying a gun himself and getting Mack to go sometime after they got back from their trip. Thinking about getting Mack a few times with paintballs put a smile on his face.

Aaron was at Justin's house when his mother called at eight in the evening. She apologized for not calling sooner and chatted endlessly for a half hour about all the sights and people there. Aaron thanked her for the $160.00 she had left for him and told her about paintball. She fretted over whether he had enough money and they hung up with I love you's.

****

Aaron arrived to church fifteen minutes early. He had had a hard time sleeping the night before and was up at the crack of dawn anxious for the day to come so he could start his journey to find his dad. He left Justin's mom believing he was going to Ralph's for a few night's and then Mike's. Justin assured him he would be home and call the cell phone number Aaron had given him if his mom called. He scanned faces looking for Mack but didn't see her. Aaron went into the church and got a seat in the third row and sat while he waited anxiously for her.

She finally arrived ten minutes after the service started to Aaron's relief and sat down in the seat he had saved for her next to Ryan, Jake and Billy. Aaron listened to the pastor speak about obedience and learned that it is so much more than the Ten Commandments. He talked about how Jesus changed everything and taught us a new way to live and how even when we aren't sure what to do, the Holy Spirit in us does. He spoke of the Holy Spirit in us and how it gives you a conscious for things when you are God's child. Your conscience helps you to know what is right from wrong, and as you grow in the Spirit, things that you normally found alright no longer are; like swearing, smoking or even gossiping or judging somebody. Aaron had a sinking feeling that his heart knew what his mind could not yet accept. His heart knew that lying and going against his parents wishes was wrong, but Aaron's mind could come up with a million reason's why his circumstance was different and therefore an exception to the rules.

Aaron and Mack left church each with a duffle bag of their stuff and headed towards Aaron's house. They decided on the way to his house after trying to get a hold of several of their friends with cars to no avail that they would get to the bus station by taxi. They figured if they faked that their parents were home the taxi driver would take them. Mack called a cab company and used her most motherly voice as she requested a taxi for her children to the bus station. When it arrived a half hour later they both stopped on the front porch with the

THE ONLY WAY HOME

door open and waved to the imaginary parent before shutting it and walked as sophisticatedly as they could to the waiting cab driver. He helped them with their bags and then confirmed that he was taking them to the bus station. When they both nodded he asked them if they had the money to pay him or if he needed to get it from their mom. They both pulled out their wads of cash and he nodded and got back in the drivers seat. They jumped quickly in the back and smiled eagerly at each other. Their journey had begun.

~15~

'Therefore, whatever you want men to do you, do also unto them, for this is the Law of the Prophets.'
Matthew 7:12 (NIV)

The yellow and white taxi-cab pulled up in front of a two story brick building with blackened windows twenty-five minutes later. Aaron and Mack emerged from the cab with bright smiles and excitement radiating from them. The overweight cab driver, who smelled slightly of onions, named Bob helped them with their bags after Aaron paid him twenty-seven dollars for the ride. They walked side by side into the building with their bags in hand. The musty, sticky smell hit Mack's face as soon as she entered. She looked around at the tiny bus station and was stunned at the lack of people in the small building, and the lack of benches. There was a long ledge along each of the walls where four people sat and looked lethargically out the windows. The center of the room was completely empty as Mack's eyes moved to the long windowed ticket taker booths where a lone man sat and smiled at them. "Don't be shy, come right up," he said with a cheerful grin. They strode over to the hefty blonde man with a beard and a Budweiser t-shirt and handed them their tickets. He told them the bus should arrive in about an hour and to wait with the others. Mack looked at Aaron wondering why they had to be there an hour early and as if reading her mind he shrugged. "After we leave here when will the first stop be?" Mack inquired.

"Your first stop will be in Detroit for an hour and forty minutes, but don't worry, it's real safe there. They have the state police the floor above them and they walk through all the time. The next stop is in Ohio and you'll probably get there a couple hours after your Detroit stop. You could be there anywhere from five to forty minutes."

"We should get some munchies and stuff then, Aaron." Mack turned back to the man behind the glass, "Is there a place close by that we can get some food to take with us?"

"Sure, if you go out the front doors and make a left, two blocks up you'll see fourth street, make a left and there's a party store right there."

"Thanks for your help." Aaron replied as they turned towards the doors.

"Anytime," the man replied as they were walking away.

When they walked into the cramped three isle party store they parted to find some snacks for the trip. They met at the check out ten minutes later each with an arm full of food and drinks. They each paid and started walking back.

"Are you scared?" Aaron asked.

"Only of getting caught."

"I've been scared for days. Scared of getting caught, scared of meeting my dad, scared of not having enough money, scared of what God thinks of me." Aaron trailed off as he stared at his Nikes.

"What do you mean? I mean I understand why you're scared of getting caught, meeting your dad and money, but what do you mean about God?"

"For a while now I have been feeling really unsettled about us going, like I'm not supposed to be doing this. I guess I'm worried about what God thinks of me. I have never really cared what anyone has ever thought, but I care what He thinks. I don't know, do you understand?"

"Not really, but I do understand that you are nervous. Aaron, you are on your way to meeting your dad for the first time. That has to be playing with your head. Anyone would be stressed out right now. Everything will be fine, you'll see." Mack threw her arm around his shoulder as they walked the last block to the bus station in silence.

When the bus finally arrived Mack, Aaron, and the other four people who were waiting boarded the bus that had six people on it already. As they were getting on the big flat faced bus they handed their bags to a man waiting by the door that took them and put them neatly in compartments underneath the bus. Aaron and Mack boarded last and got two adjacent seats in the very last row. They were eager to be on their way and Aaron's trepidation gave way to adrenaline as the bus finally heaved onto Lafayette. They both peered out the windows in silence as they made their way to Detroit.

The sights changed dramatically from nice suburbs to inner city within twenty minutes. They had both been to Detroit before for hockey and baseball games, but never really looked at it like they did now. Aaron noticed how the houses went from nice with spacious well groomed yards, to duplexes, some abandoned and boarded up. There was a sense of foreboding in him as he watched the traffic get thicker as they got closer. Then they saw the high rise buildings come into view. They both smiled and pointed to the Renaissance Center building, then Comerica Park. They saw people filing in and out of the Hockeytown Café and Mack's face lit up as she pointed and told Aaron how much she wanted to go there during a Stanley Cup game to watch the Red Wings play. "It must get wild in there during the playoffs," she stated emphatically. Aaron couldn't help but smile at her enthusiasm as their bus slowed to a stop in front of the Detroit bus station.

They were only less than an hour away from home and already it looked as if they had entered a whole new world. There were business men and women, blue and white collar, kids trying to keep up with their mom as she hurried down the bustling city street, couples lazily strolling holding hands. They were making their way into the new bus station after the skinny brown eyed female driver told them that they could leave their bags because they would be boarding this bus again in an hour or so.

This bus station was quite different from the last one. It was much larger and there was between thirty and forty people waiting for a bus or someone to pick them up. This one actually had benches, lockers, and vending machines like Mack had expected to see at the last one. There was a huge diversity in the people as well. Every ethnicity and color was present. They walked quickly to the corner holding their bags of food and their small carry-ons that they each had taken.

Mack sat close to Aaron as she looked around apprehensively. She nudged Aaron with her elbow when she realized a man who was obviously homeless, wearing tattered clothes, mismatched shoes, and a dirty torn Lion's baseball hat that barely hid his un-kept hair, met her gaze and started walking towards them. His wild, nearly black eyes were piercing as he smiled at her. When Aaron just nudged her back, she shoved him hard and he howled as he grabbed his now bruised upper arm. His eyes met hers as he was about to let out an explicative but didn't when he noticed the fear in her expressive eyes. She tilted her head and he followed the direction of her eyes towards the almost stumbling homeless man now only just a few feet away. She latched on to his arm as the man came to a weaving halt just in front of them. "Got any money I could have? I'm a vet ya know." The man smelled of liquor and was shaking as he put out his hand for them to give him something.

"We don't have much," Aaron said as he rose and dug into his pockets for the change he had put there from the party store. "But I'll buy you something from the vending machine if you are hungry." The man looked disgruntled and continued holding out his hand for the money.

"What?! You think I can't buy my own food from a machine? Or maybe you don't think I'll buy food with it?" The man's voice grew a couple of octaves as he stood before them unmoved by their gesture. He was in the process of taking a step closer to Aaron when a police man grabbed the man by the arm. "I told you I didn't want to see you in here again hassling people Joe. These kids were going to buy you a bite to eat and you couldn't even be nice enough to accept it. Now you get on over to the mission and find a warm bed tonight, okay?" The homeless man named Joe mumbled something and started to make his way to the doors of the bus station without a backwards glance. The police man had kind eyes as he apologized for Joe and then asked them if they were alone.

~16~

*'Children, obey your parents in the Lord, for this is right.
"Honor your father and mother"-which is the first
commandment with a promise-'
Ephesians 6:1-2 (NIV)*

"Yes, we are on our way to our grandma's in Pensacola," Mack stated hoping he wouldn't ask any more questions.
"Well, you guys stay close to each other and be careful."
"We will, and thank you for helping with that guy."
The nice policeman said, "Sure," without turning around and headed towards the elevators.
Aaron watched Joe open the doors to the bus station, shake his head and start walking through them. Aaron asked God to help Joe find Him and also that God would help him find his place in this world so that he can take care of himself. Mack heard Aaron mumbling with his eyes shut and nudged him to find out what he was doing. "Who are you talking to?"
"I was praying that God would help Joe." He answered without looking at her.
"Why? He was completely rude to us."
"God still loves him." She didn't have a reply to that as she watched Aaron pull out his walkman.

The next hour went by without incident, Aaron and Mack sat reading magazines while eating pretzels and sipping on pops waiting for their bus number to be called. When it finally did they were surprised that the bus was less than half full. They took the very last row of seats for themselves and got comfortable for their long journey.

****

Aaron was dreaming that he and Mack had gotten separated and she needed him, but he couldn't find her when he was jolted awake by the bus coming to an abrupt halt. He bolted upright in his seat and looked over to see Mack still sleeping. He let out a deep breathe that he didn't even realize he had been holding in. He yawned as he realized he had actually gotten some sleep. Mack had become car sick a few hours into their trip and they both had been up most of the night. He rubbed the sleep from his eyes and looked out of the bus window. The bus had the air conditioner on and the sun looked bright in the clear blue sky. They were stopped at a mini plaza with a gas station, Subway, and a store. "We must've come a long way," he said more to himself than anyone else. He glanced at his watch to see the time was just after the noon hour and peered down the isle to see the other few passengers doing the same.

Aaron saw the smoke then. A huge billow of black smoke was rising from the front of the bus. "Anyone know what's going on?" Aaron called towards the front of the bus to anyone who cared to answer. "Looks like we broke down," the reply came from a large construction worker looking guy in his fifties who was wearing faded jeans, a flannel shirt and a geeky welder's cap that was navy with white poke-a-dots. The hat sat entirely too high on his head, but covered his receding hairline well.

Aaron shook Mack and she slowly came awake. He told her the bus broke down and she sat straight up to look out the window. The bus driver who had gotten out of the bus came back in and announced that he would have to radio for another bus to come and get them because this one was obviously having some engine problems. A few of the passengers grumbled and asked how long it would be and the driver told them when he knew, he would let them know.

The passengers started getting up and moving off of the bus to stretch their legs and eat. When Mack and Aaron emerged from the bus, toting their carry-ons, they stopped to get in line behind a few people who were waiting to retrieve their bags from the bottom of the bus. "Why are we getting our luggage now? It could be a while before another bus gets here."

"I'd like to change and freshen up, don't you?" Mack asked back.

"Good point. We are almost there, you feel any better today?"

"When I don't have to take any more of that Dramamine, I'll be great. It's so warm out now I want to put some shorts on, I feel like I'm melting. It must be 85 degrees out here." Mack tilted her face up and let the sun warm her face. Aaron watched her and smiled.

When they entered the doors to the Subway they realized the store and gas station were all connected in one building with it. "This is different," Aaron commented as he strode into the men's room. Mack smiled as she went down the opposite hallway to the women's room. When she reached the door she stopped short and stared at a bright yellow sign on it that read 'SORRY – OUT OF ORDER'. Mack gaped stupidly at the sign for a full minute before sighing and walking back to wait for Aaron. A few minutes later Aaron emerged wearing cargo shorts and a dark green t-shirt. "Why didn't you change?"

"The bathroom is out of order. I need to ask where to go. Just wait for me in here. I'll be back in a few."

"Alright, do you want me to get you a sandwich?"

"No that's okay, I'll get one when I get back. I'm only gonna be gone a minute."

"Okay, I'll be here."

Mack walked over to the young girl behind the cash register and asked if there was another bathroom that she could use.

"Yeah, you just gotta walk around back to the employee bathroom because it's against store policy to let you through our storage area." Mack smiled at the woman as she thanked her and turned to leave.

When she rounded the back of the building she looked for the door to the employee bathroom and noticed a small brown building with no windows and a white door connected to the back of the plaza and assumed she had found it. She turned the knob gingerly and was happy she didn't have to wait for anyone in the sweltering heat. After she had changed and taken care of the necessities she started back to find Aaron. She had made it half way there when a heavy set man who looked like he hadn't shaved in a week called out to her from his rig some twenty feet away at a pump. She stopped and looked at him inquiringly until she realized he wasn't just saying hello. "Hey baby, need someone to take care of you? Where are you going?" The obese man yelled out to her again as she turned and started a fast walk towards the store.

She was nearly running when she got to the doors and spotted Aaron quickly, sitting at a booth near the entrance. "What's wrong?" Aaron asked.

"This horrible man was yelling at me on my way back, it spooked me a little, I'm okay." Aaron looked appalled and asked where he was. "It's okay really. I'm just not going to take anymore strolls around rest stops alone." Aaron grunted and started eating again as Mack went to the counter to order something for herself.

Aaron sat barely stomaching the food he knew he should be hungry for. It seemed the farther they got on their journey, the more sick he felt in the pit of his stomach. He tried to blame it on nerves because with each mile they made on their trip it was a mile closer to his father, but knew deep down it was something much more than that.

~17~

'Then they cried out to the Lord in their trouble, and he delivered them from their distress.'
Psalm 107:6 (NIV)

Aaron and Mack decided to go and see if there was any news yet on the arrival of the replacement bus. They boarded the bus and found the bus driver reclined in the first row of seats reading a John Grisham novel, a bag of chips in his lap. "Excuse me sir, is there any word yet on when we will be able to get out of here?"

"Yeah, looks like we are going to be here for a while. The guy is on his way but looks like he won't be here till sometime between ten and eleven tonight. We are going to hitch a ride with another group on their way to Pensacola." The bus driver shrugged, never taking his eyes off of his book. Aaron and Mack took a long look at each other and sighed.

"Georgia isn't that bad is it?" The construction worker asked taking in their long faces as he passed them with a coke in hand retreating back into the air conditioning of the bus. Mack and Aaron smiled in unison at the friendly man and continued walking passed him. "So what do we do now?" Mack looked bored already.

"I guess just hang out and make the best of it." Aaron tried to be positive.

They settled down with their magazines in the sub shop and tried to pass the time. By dinner time the flow of traffic through the tiny establishment had picked up substantially. There was every different kind of person coming through for gas or a snack. 'People watching' became their favorite pass time throughout the day. It's amazing how much you can see about a person just by watching them for a few minutes. There was a couple fighting, oblivious to their audience. Old people coming for the ice cream that was on sale, young locals who rode their bikes up to hang out.

They were settled in their booth both lost in their own thoughts when Aaron stood up. "Be right back, the pop went right through me."

"T.M.I. hun," Mack smiled as she turned to the ringing of the obnoxious bell above the door to the sub shop signaling a new arrival.

"T.M.I.?"

"Too much information." Aaron chuckled as he turned to use the facilities.

Mack noticed two seventeen to eighteen year old boys enter wearing black bandanas over their hair that was entirely too long. They looked around before turning their attention to the menu that was written on poster board and taped high on the wall behind the counter. The shorter of the two, sporting faded ripped jeans that looked four sizes too big and hung low enough to reveal his teal polka-dotted boxers, nudged his companion. The taller boy turned his attention to him obviously annoyed. Mack cringed as she realized they had noticed her looking at them. She directed her gaze to the magazine that lay long forgotten on the table. She watched them through her peripheral vision as they left the line and started towards her.

The two stopped directly in front of her booth as she pretended not to notice their arrival. "Hey sweet thing, what's up?" She couldn't pretend not to notice them any longer. "We got some good stuff in the van, why don't you come party with us for a bit. If you don't have enough cash we could figure something else out." The two looked at each other exchanging knowing smiles.

Her face must have turned crimson if the heat radiating from her face was any indication. She stood and for the first time looked them in the eye. "Why don't you two take your combined IQ of 19 and get lost." They looked momentarily stunned at her outburst, and then a bit put out.

"You ungrateful hussy! There isn't one girl in this town that wouldn't jump at the offer we just gave you."

"What, so all four of them like you two? That doesn't impress me much." She knew she was playing with fire, but was having too much fun to care. Aaron got back to the table his eyes trained on Mack. "What's going on?"

"You ought to keep her on a leash, there is a few things I would do with her nasty mouth to preoccupy it." The shorter boy received a high five from his cohort for that little come back. Aaron quickly understood the situation and put himself between Mackenzie and the two boys who were now starting to lean closer.

"Look man you need to back off. Seriously we aren't looking for trouble but if you insult my friend again we are going to have a problem." Aaron was feeling the familiar knot starting to form in the pit of his stomach. He didn't care if they were older or larger, or even if he would win. It just seemed right to inflict some kind of repercussion for treating Mackenzie the way they did.

The taller boy lifted his shirt a few inches to reveal a black gun tucked in the front of his jeans. Aaron swallowed hard, for the first time in his life he was truly scared. Mack didn't see the unspoken exchange between Aaron and the tall boy and was still glaring at the two over Aaron's shoulder. "Is there a problem here?" The deep voice came from behind the two boys. They all swiveled around in unison and saw the big burly construction worker from the bus with the welding cap. Aaron sighed relief as the two boys started backing away from them.

"No man, we were just leaving," the shorter boy replied as he glared at Aaron. They both turned and started towards the door.

"Thank you," Aaron replied.

"If you two need anything, don't be afraid to holler. There are a lot of nut jobs out and about, can't be too careful." With that he left and headed towards the still waiting bus. Aaron watched the older man exit the building and his eyes were drawn to a rusted old van parked just outside the window. The two teenagers were standing by their respective car doors lip sinking 'We're waiting for you'. A chill ran down Aaron's spine as a sense of foreboding came over him.

"What jerks!" Mackenzie stated the obvious as she made a rude gesture to the now departing van.

"They had a gun and I have a really bad feeling that they are going to come back." Aaron didn't hide the apprehension in his voice.

"What?!" Mack's face lost its pallor as she realized they were in very real danger.

"We have got to get out of here."

"What exactly are you thinking?"

"If we see that van again we are going to walk across the overpass to that other truck stop until the other bus gets here."

"Why not just get on the bus now?"

"If they are as stupid as they appeared to be I wouldn't want to put anyone on the bus at risk of being hurt."

"What about the cops?"

"And tell them what when we aren't of age to make a statement and they ask to speak to our parents?"

After an hour of watching the parking lot without blinking they both started to relax. Aaron started to look through his duffle bag for more reading material as Mackenzie got up to dispose of their garbage from the food they had eaten. On her way back to the table she froze as if seeing a ghost in the middle of the room. Aaron looked up at her and taking in her expression turned his attention in the direction of what held her captivated.

The rusty van was pulling into a parking spot to the right of the building and there were at least two more occupants than the first time it had been here. Aaron grabbed both duffle bags as he started towards a still frozen Mackenzie. He took her hand and started towards the gas station side of the building where he remembered seeing a side door out into the parking lot. He pulled her in his wake as he made his way quickly through the doors. The parking lot was well lit and Aaron and Mackenzie ran as fast as they could towards the woods that loomed like a scene from a scary movie in the darkness of the night.

They ran into the safety the woods offered without looking back. They moved quickly through the thick foliage hand in hand. Mack tripped over an exposed tree root and fell hard. She yelled out in pain and looked down at her now bleeding right knee. Aaron came down beside her and assessed the damage as they both tried to catch their breath.
They both heard it at the same time. Someone was in the woods with them. They could hear the rustling of the underbrush and voices. Their eyes met and neither had to say what they were thinking. "I can't run anymore I think I messed up my knee pretty bad." Mack started to cry as she peered desperately into the darkness trying to figure out which direction the boys were coming from.
"We'll have to hide then. Let me help you." Aaron tried to help Mack to her feet, but ended up carrying her altogether when she almost fell again. Aaron was strong for his size but two duffle bags and a fifteen year old girl seemed to be a bit much after a few yards. He spotted an ideal location in between a large rock and a prickly bush and sat her down there. They huddled together listening for anymore noises, both praying for help. They were getting eaten alive by

mosquitoes when they stopped breathing because they heard someone moving closer to their hiding spot. Aaron wrapped his arms around Mackenzie and tucked her head down against his chest trying to make himself a shield to protect her from whatever may be coming for them. He prayed. He prayed harder than he has ever prayed before. 'Lord, please protect us. I know this was a mistake, and I am so sorry. Please don't let anything happen to her, she shouldn't even be here. Lord please, please.'

The form of the person making the noise came into view and Aaron readied himself to do whatever it would take to protect them. He kept a constant prayer going in his head as he peered through the bush at the tall boy who stopped to take a break from looking for them by resting on the boulder they were hiding behind. He could hear other voices as the boy on the rock called out to his friends. Mack was shaking and breathing hard so Aaron held her tighter trying to calm her. Aaron knew they were moments away from being spotted.

All four boys now were within two feet of their hiding spot smoking cigarettes and cursing into the night. Every once in a while they would yell out 'We're coming for you!' Aaron was still praying as the boys made their way as a group away from where they were hiding back towards the gas station some twenty minutes later.

"How did they not see us?"

"I don't know, lets just stay quiet and wait here a little longer then we can try and get back to the bus okay?" Mack stayed huddled with her head resting on his shoulder and nodded.

They made it back to the gas station almost forty minutes later and Aaron scanned the parking lot for the van before leaving the safety of the trees. "I think they're gone, got some bad news though." Mack looked up and groaned. "Our bus is gone too."

"What?! They can't just leave, can they?"

"Apparently they can. Should we go try and find a ride at the truck stop on the other side of the overpass?"

"Do we have any other options?"

~18~

'Now go; I will help you speak and teach you what to say.'
Exodus 4:12 (NIV)

Aaron helped Mackenzie walk along the side of the two lane street, both feeling defeated. "Is it me or did they totally see us." Mack looked up at Aaron.

"They did, I know they did."

"I don't get it."

Aaron stopped walking and set his bag down. He prayed silently that God would help him and give him the words that she needed to hear so that she would come to Him.

"The entire time we were trying to get away I was praying Mack, praying that He would help us."

"Me too." Her statement wasn't lost on Aaron.

"Haven't you ever heard of missionaries in foreign countries that are about to be attacked by rival tribes? And as they watch from their huts the tribe that was most definitely coming to slaughter them, turns and leaves. Then when everything calms down they asked them why they didn't kill them and they said there was an army in front of their dwelling, so they left. But the missionaries never saw a soul outside. I even heard of a couple of girls who were leaving the mall late and when they were heading to their car two men started to chase them. They ran and when they made it to their car the girls got in and locked it. They tried to start the car as the men who were after them, for who knows what, pounded on their windows. The car wouldn't start, so the girl's prayed and then tried again. The car started the second time and the girls raced home. The next day the girl's father checked the engine to see why it wouldn't start, and when he realized the battery had been removed he was astounded. It is impossible to start a car without a battery. There is no explanation how the tribe saw an army that over twenty people claim wasn't there, or why a car would start without the battery. Miracles do happen." Aaron let his words sink in as Mack sat across from him, mosquitoes forgotten, staring intently at something over his right shoulder.

"But we aren't missionaries, I'm not even religious." Her eyes welled up with unshed tears, she felt as though for the first time in her life she was being loved and protected the way she always wished she could be. Something inside of her was breaking and she didn't even try to hold back her emotions as she started to sob uncontrollably.

"*We* are still His children. Even though you haven't asked Him into your life yet, He still has His hand on you Mack. He has been with you your whole life, waiting for you to accept Him. The bible said that even greater things than Jesus did, we would do. If you believe that He loves you, then why wouldn't He protect you?" Aaron knew the feeling Mack was experiencing as he waited for her to get a hold of herself again. Aaron had felt the same way when he and Ryan had had the same conversation.

"I'm so scared that if I put all my hope in Him that I'm going to get let down. I have gotten let down my whole life," she said a few minutes later, as her tears fell silently down her cheeks.

"That's the whole wonderful thing about it. You have to have faith. If you believe in Him, that means you believe in His word. The two are intertwined, if you don't believe what He says, then you don't believe in Him, and he says He won't ever let you down. He cannot tell a lie,

THE ONLY WAY HOME

and what He says has to happen." He sat silently staring at her waiting for her to speak.

"I want to do it. How do I?" She couldn't finish as she began to cry again.

"Just repeat after me." Aaron led her through the sinner's prayer. She repeated each word that Aaron said as she kneeled in the dirt on the side of the road her head in her hands. When they finished they sat there some time drinking water and talking of what was to come.

They made it to the truck stop and looked around apprehensively at the rows and rows of parked semis. "I think we should pray before we look to find the person to ask." They held hands and prayed together and then walked into the building that housed a restaurant, bathrooms and a gas station. They entered the small diner and sat down so Aaron could inspect Mackenzie's knee. Mackenzie looked around speculatively at the people in the building and none of them seemed safe to her.

Aaron stated, "I think you just twisted it a little. It isn't swelling at all." A look of relief crossed his face.

"It doesn't hurt nearly as much as it did. My hockey coach isn't going to kill me, that's a good thing," Mackenzie teased trying to lighten Aaron's mood. "We will just wait until we see someone who looks decent, I guess."

Aaron looked deflated as he scanned the room, "Coffee?"

"You know I don't drink coffee."

"Looks like we are going to be here for a while now might be a good time to start."

Aaron and Mackenzie both sat in the booth for what seemed like an eternity when a man walked in carrying a book called 'Chicken Soup for the Christian Soul'. They both eyed him as Aaron nodded to Mack. "I'm not asking, you ask," Mack stated. "This was your idea."

"Yeah, but I think if a girl asks he will be more likely to do it," Aaron said still looking at the man.

"You are on something if you think I am going over there," she replied with finality.

They were both surprised when the man walked over to them, hands on hips looking them over. "Ask me what?"

"Um... we uh, were looking to get a ride to Pensacola sir, and um we thought you might help us." Aaron finished while looking at his feet.

"Well, I'm headed to St. Petersburg, but I guess we could swing by there. It's not really out of my way. What are you kids doing out here hitch hiking?" He was staring from Mack to Aaron.

"Our bus broke down and we are on our way to my dad's," Aaron replied finally meeting his stare.

"He knows you are here hitchhiking?"

"No sir. I am surprising him with this visit."

The man looked Aaron and Mackenzie over a long while, "Well, alright then. I am leaving after I grab a coffee, you ready?" Mack and Aaron nodded simultaneously and followed the white haired man out of the diner.

They made it to Pensacola, enjoying the man and his easy going conversation. They showed him the address of Aaron's father and he took them to within three blocks of it. They exited the rig and thanked the man named Don for all of his help. He brushed off their appreciation with a stern warning not to hitch rides from anyone again. They both smiled and waved as he pulled his massive truck back into traffic.

"We made it, we are in Pensacola." Mack said excitedly. She was on the verge of skipping if only her knee would stop throbbing. They walked the three blocks to the address Aaron had and stood there on the steps of the large apartment complex. Aaron's mind raced between running away and running inside. He was shaking and trying to remember to how to breathe when he thought it might be better to wait until tomorrow.

~19~

'Turn your ear to me, come quickly to my rescue; be my rock of refuge, a strong fortress to save me.'
Psalm 31:2 (NIV)

Aaron stood at the top step staring at the list of names and corresponding apartment numbers, contemplating whether or not to ring the buzzer. "Maybe we should get a room somewhere and something to eat before we do this," Aaron said still looking at the buzzer marked thirty-four, the one that would announce his arrival to his father.

"We'll probably end up staying here, dummy. But there is a little deli over there that I am going to go to while you guys talk. Just come and get me when… you know." She smiled at him then started across the street towards the deli. Aaron only shook his head.

Aaron stood a long time praying that God would give him courage. He looked around at the run down apartment building and sighed. He didn't feel much better when he finished, but he knew he wasn't alone and that was all the encouragement he needed to ring the door buzzer. He waited a few minutes and then rang it again. An annoyed voice resounded from the speaker below the buttons. "What?!"

"Um yes, is this Tony Guarez?"

"Who wants to know?" There was a slight accent in his voice.

"Um, would it be okay if I came up to talk to you?" Aaron's stomach was turning and he felt as if he might loose his resolve.

"No. Whatever you are selling I don't want any."

"I'm not selling anything. My name is Aaron. Please I have traveled a long way to find you. May I see you?"

"Larry sent you, eh? You tell Larry that he'll have his money in a week like I said."

"I don't know any Larry." Aaron felt defeated and decided to just tell him even though he wanted to be face to face. "I'm Aaron McKay, you're my father." Aaron held his breath as he waited for his response. There was none, just the resounding loud buzz and click of the door being unlocked.

Aaron made his way up the stairs to the third floor carefully avoiding the empty pizza boxes and beer cans that littered the hallways. He found the door with a thirty-four written on it with marker and knocked softly. The door opened wide and a man with the same jet black wavy hair as his stood before him. Aaron's eyes went wide at the tall man with broad shoulders and full lips staring down at him. He realized he was gaping at the man and turned his attention to his cut off shorts, and ripped tank top, revealing strong shoulders and muscular arms. He had a tattoo of a naked lady on his forearm. Aaron dropped his duffel bag as the smell of beer radiating from him hit Aaron's nostrils. "So what is it you want?"

Aaron's eyes flew to his. "I just wanted to meet you."

"Yeah okay, look I'm broke and I ain't got nuthin' for ya." Tony eyed Aaron and Aaron felt as if he was shrinking.

"No, you don't understand. I don't want anything from you. I traveled here all the way from Michigan because I wanted to meet you."

"Well, here I am. I am not now and never was looking to be a dad, that's what I told your mom and that's what I am telling you. Look kid, I have to be at a new job at the plant in an hour so anything else you wanted to say?" Tony looked bored as he leaned his large body against the door frame.

Aaron felt fury building inside of him as he looked at his long lost dad who was obviously drunk by the smell of him. "Actually there is something I wanted to say. I cannot believe my own stupidity in coming all the way here for someone as sorry as you. Do you realize I have spent most of my life dreaming of you and what would happen to my life if only I could have found you? For some reason I thought you would be the answer to everything wrong in my life, but instead you just added to it. Have a nice life." Aaron picked up his duffel bag as he turned and walked away from his father without a backward glance. As Aaron stood on the steps to the apartment building looking across the street towards the deli he realized he had just written his father out of his life as easily as his father had done to him so many years before.

~20~

'In my anguish I cried to the Lord, and he answered by setting me free.'
Psalm 118:5 (NIV)

    Aaron sat down on the steps to the apartment complex his whole body racking with sobs. He folded his arms around his head as he gave into all of the anxiety, fear, and disappointment he felt. He vaguely heard people coming and leaving the apartments and didn't have a doubt in his mind that if his father had been one of the people leaving he wouldn't have given him a second glance. His mind cried out to the Lord in confusion. 'Why did he have to be that way? Why did I feel like this is what I was supposed to do? Lord, please help me understand.'
    As soon as he thought those words, the dreams he had had came to the front of his mind. The dreams where he had been so safe with his father, seeing wondrous things and feeling so secure. The Lord whispered into his mind 'in those dreams you were always with Me'. Aaron's mind reeled at the new understanding. He looked up to the perfectly crystal blue sky and wiped the tears from his face and felt a cool breeze. 'Why did I feel like this was what I was supposed to do Lord? You have to tell me when I am wrong so that I don't ever

make a mistake like this again.' Aaron's mind immediately thought of the dream he had had about being in a desert with the sweltering heat and he had seen an oasis, beckoning him to indulge in its cool waters, and when he had dove in it, it wasn't real. He remembered the feeling of complete desolation he had felt and shivered. He also thought of Ryan and how he had tried to warn him about what he was going to do and how he had lost control and gotten into a fight with him. He remembered the pastor on the TV saying 'seek your father, knock and the door will open,' and smiled to himself at how God was trying to tell him to seek after *Him*.

Aaron could not explain his mood as he walked, head high across the street to the deli where Mackenzie waited for him. 'I should be so upset and mad right now' he thought to himself. 'But I'm not, I feel as though for the first time in my life I am alright. I'm not searching for something that was never there to begin with, and that's okay, because what I do have is so much better'.

****

Aaron and Mack settled into the large bus that was going to take them home. They had each called again to make sure their cover had not been blown and as far as they could tell everything was going as planned. Mack could not believe her friends faith but yearned for it. "If I could have faith like yours I don't think anything I could ever go through would be too hard." Mack said after several minutes of silence. Aaron smiled at her and said, "You already do, you just don't know it yet."

****

They arrived in Michigan on Thursday at 4:20 pm. Aaron got on the cell phone to see if Ryan would pick them up. When there was no answer they got a cab and headed back to Aaron's house. They arrived a half hour later Aaron was shocked to see his mother's minivan in the driveway. "Aaron, what's going on?" Mack said taking in his expression.

"My mom isn't supposed to be here till Saturday. Her car wasn't there when we left." Aaron retrieved their bags and handed Mack hers as he told her to go home. Mack paid the cab driver and whispered 'good luck' as she made her way through the yards.

Aaron didn't even make it onto the porch when his mother came through the front door and ran to him tears streaming down her pale face. Aaron noticed the dark smudges under her eyes from lack of sleep and immediately felt intense guilt at what she must've gone through not knowing where he was. "Oh my God! You're okay! Oh my God, thank you for bringing him home!" She was hugging him and kissing him like he was a child all over his face, while his stepfather stood a few feet away. He noticed then that Ben looked just as haggard his mother did. Aaron stared at the other man a long time while his mother got her fill of holding him again. When she finally pulled away he stood before the proud man he had never before given a chance to be a father to him because he was so obsessed with finding his real dad. A tear slipped out as Aaron realized the gift he had been given in Ben. He walked over to him as Ben stood trying to swallow the lump in his throat and hugged him for the very first time.

They talked for a long while about what had happened. Aaron shared how God had changed his life and how sorry he was for what he had done. Aaron's mother told him how if she only knew he wanted to meet his dad she would have helped him, regardless of the fact that she knew Aaron would be disappointed. Aaron agreed not to keep anything like that from her again, and she seemed to be appeased. He still got grounded for a month, but felt as though that was a small price to pay for what he had learned.

That evening while he and his parents were watching the news Aaron almost came off of the couch when he saw the face of the homeless man he had met at the Detroit bus station. He was shaved and dressed in a suit as he spoke. Aaron couldn't believe the transformation of the man he had met. He looked almost like Denzel Washington when he was cleaned up. He grabbed the remote from Ben and said he'd explain in a minute as he turned the volume up and gaped open-mouthed at the man before him on TV. Aaron listened as he spoke. "My life changed forever when my wife and two sons died in a car accident twelve years ago. My wife Charlotte and I had been married for eight years and Johnny and Phillip were just six and four when on that January morning I was driving them to breakfast and we collided with a SUV that had lost control on the icy street. I was a marketing executive for a computer company at the time and I think I just lost any reason I had ever had to live. I stopped going to work and lost my house and well, here I am." The man was trying to keep his face neutral while he told of the hardships in his life, but his eyes betrayed him.

The newscaster asked, "Well, tell us how everything changed four days ago." Aaron mentally counted back in his head and realized the day everything changed for that man was the same day he and Mack had met him.

"I was on my way back to the shelter when a guy that was buying a newspaper asked if I had been wearing my shoes long. I was wearing two different sneakers at the time, and told him three years. He was interested in which one felt better and lasted longer. When I told him he told me he was an executive for that sneakers company and he was very interested in doing commercials and advertising with me, a guy that really knew which was the better shoe."

"So your life was changed because of your shoes… amazing."

The man cut in. "No it wasn't the shoes. When my family was taken from me I turned my back on God. A few nights before this all happened I asked God for forgiveness and I believed He would help me put my life back together. I guess this is the way he is putting it back for me."

Aaron lay in bed that night feeling more content than he had ever remembered when the phone rang. He heard Ryan's voice and smiled, he was so excited to tell his friend all that had happened to him. "Aaron, I have been trying to call you all week." Ryan's voice sounded strained and weak.

"Are you okay, your voice sounds funny?"

"Aaron, I'm in the hospital. I tried to call you."

Aaron's eyes burned as he sat straight up in bed and tried to clear his head, realizing something was very wrong. "I am not doing so well."

"That's okay Ryan, when are you getting out?" Aaron was trying to make his voice sound light as he reeled inside.

"I don't think I am coming home this time, Aaron."

~21~

'Hear my prayer, O Lord, Give ear to my supplications! In Your faithfulness answer me, And in Your righteousness.'
Psalm 143:1 (NKJ)

Aaron sat shaking his head, he wouldn't believe that. "Yes you are, don't talk like that. You are going to be just fine! With God anything is possible, right?" Aaron tried to think positively but he was having a hard time.

"I'm getting worse and have stopped responding to treatment. Don't worry, everything will be okay. God has given me peace, I'm not scared." Ryan's voice sounded confident even though it was a raspy whisper. Aaron swallowed back tears at the finality of Ryan's words. Why would this happen to such a good person? Why would God let someone who loves Him as much as Ryan does die? It didn't make any sense to Aaron. "What hospital are you at? I'm coming to see you."

****

Aaron told Ben what was happening with Ryan. When he asked him to drive him to the hospital he finally broke down. Ben held him tight and tried to offer what little comfort he could. "I know this is hard, but from everything you have told your mother and me about your faith, it should give you comfort to know that God has a plan for everyone." Aaron nodded into his chest and prayed silently for Ryan and understanding.

Aaron sat next to Ryan's hospital bed as his friend slept. He looked around the room at all of the monitors and machines giving medicine and felt small and helpless. Ryan's family was in the corridor and peeked in on them every few minutes. Aaron felt bad for taking time away from them to be with Ryan, but was grateful for the few minutes he had been given to be alone with his friend. He felt a warm hand touch his and looked down to see Ryan's hand on his. He looked at his warm brown eyes and choked back a sob. He was so pale and fragile it hurt to look at him. "It will be okay," was all he said before falling back to sleep.

Aaron knelt in his room with the door locked for the rest of that day. Mackenzie had called for him and Aaron's mother explained what was happening to Ryan and that Aaron wanted to be left alone. Mack asked Beth to let Aaron know she would pray for Ryan and him. Beth assured her that she would and that Aaron would call her as soon as he could.

Aaron was planning on going back to the hospital the following morning and was determined to pray for some sign that Ryan would be okay by the time he saw him again, and he wasn't going to stop praying until he got it. He prayed with everything that he had inside of him, he wept, and he pleaded, and even bargained with God. He offered anything he could think of in exchange for Ryan to be made better. Aaron fell into exhaustion on the floor of his room several hours into the late night still pleading for a sign that Ryan would be okay.

****

Aaron awoke in the early afternoon to the light from his window streaming all around him warming his skin. He rubbed his eyes as he pulled himself off of the floor. He stumbled towards his door and was unlocking it when he noticed a piece of paper that had been slid under his door. He picked it up and it read:

I wanted to make sure that you knew I will be okay.
God brought to my heart a verse that I wanted to share with you.
"And God will wipe away every tear from their eyes; there shall be
no more death, nor sorrow, nor crying. There shall be no more pain,
for the former things have passed away."

Aaron wept as he read his answered prayer. He smiled in his heart at the words he had spoke to Ryan so long ago about God answering prayers by slipping notes under doors, because that's exactly what had just happened. Even though it was his mother's handwriting and Ryan's message, Aaron knew it was God's answer.

Aaron came down the stairs with a feeling of relief until he saw his mother and Ben at the table. The look on their faces stopped his heart as he started shaking his head. Aaron's mother started towards him with her hands stretched out to comfort him as she said, "Aaron it happened early this morning, Ryan's mom called me an hour after Ryan did to give you that message." Aaron felt the room spin as he dropped to his knees.

~22~

'The Lord is good to all; He has compassion on all He has made.'
Psalm 145:9 (NIV)

Aaron wept like a child in his mother's arms on the floor of the kitchen. Ben knelt behind Aaron, his hand resting on his shoulder as Aaron's body racked with sobs. "I prayed mom, I prayed so hard. It didn't matter. I thought the note from Ryan meant he was going to be okay. Why?" Aaron bit out between sobs.

"Sometimes it's better. He doesn't have to suffer anymore, Aaron." His mother softly said as she continued to rock him. He pulled away from her and God at the same instant. He stood his face hardening, eyes clearing. "Why should I put my faith in a God who would let this happen to someone He is supposed to love? He is playing sick jokes with me, making me think one thing then having it be completely different." Aaron turned on his last word at his parents stunned looks and stormed back to his room which was now his hiding place.

Aaron stayed in his room for the next two days barely eating the food his mother put outside his door. His parents tried to talk to him but he wouldn't allow anyone into the isolation he put himself in. The isolation felt better than trying to deal with how he was feeling inside. Mackenzie had come to his house every day wanting to talk with him, but he wouldn't allow even her into this place.

****

Aaron dressed for the funeral in his only suit and walked numbly to his awaiting parents who were accompanying him to the church. The conversation was one-sided on the way to the church as Aaron stared out the window of the minivan trying to swallow all that he felt.

They arrived to a jammed parking lot with throngs of people entering the church making it close to impossible to navigate the parking lot. Aaron was amazed at how many people were coming to pay their respects to his friend.

As they entered the church a new pang of feeling came over him as he saw Mack standing by the wide double doors to the sanctuary with her mother in a black skirt with matching jacket, her long hair pulled back into a pony tail. The two friends walked towards each other and embraced. It was all Aaron could do not to break down. He didn't want to be comforted. He pulled out of her arms and stared into her now tear-filled eyes. "I am sorry I haven't been able to see you, I really needed some time to think all this through."

"I understand, are you okay?" Her concern for him was written all over her face.

Aaron bit back hard a fresh feeling of rage at that statement. All he wanted from God was to know if Ryan would be okay, and God lied. "Fine," he managed. "Where is your dad?"

"He checked himself into a rehabilitation center last night." Aaron hugged her again and felt relief that her family would be okay. "You sure our parents should be walking together seeing you got away with all this?" Mack smirked up at him and they both laughed. A hand touched Aaron's shoulder and he turned to see Gus standing next to him in a sweater and dark jeans.

"Look man, I am sorry," was all he had to say as they shook hands and Gus moved in front of them and into the sanctuary.

Mackenzie and Aaron walked together as their parents trailed behind them into the sanctuary where there was now standing room only, so they made there way to an empty spot along the wall.

Aaron stared blankly in front of him not really listening as the youth pastor John talked to the filled room. After John finished, one by one people who were closest to Ryan came to the podium to share a memory or how they felt with the crowd. After two hours of person after person speaking Aaron started to realize how much of a life Ryan had already led, how many lives he had touched. It wasn't just family speaking anymore, it was his friends. The kids from the soccer team, people who had found God because of him at the food drive he helped with. All of these people were touched by God through him in some way.

Aaron felt something break inside of him as he let the tears stream down his cheeks. He knew now what God had been telling him and pulled away from the wall and started towards the front of the sanctuary. When he reached the front he took his place in the line of people waiting to say something about Ryan.

As he walked up the steps to the podium and turned to face the mass of people all looking at him with understanding and acceptance he felt a peace wash over him and began to speak. "I haven't known Ryan as long as most of you have, but in the short time I have, he had become one of my closest friends. He brought me to God by the person that he was. He was a rock in my life that I never thought I'd have to live without.

I prayed all night on Friday for God to give me a sign that Ryan was going to be okay. I pleaded and begged and bartered with Him to let him be okay. When I woke up on Saturday there was a note under my door," Aaron said, pulling the note out of his pocket. "It said, 'I wanted to make sure that you knew I will be okay. God brought to my heart a verse that I wanted to share with you. 'And God will wipe away every tear from their eyes; there shall be no more death, nor sorrow, nor crying. There shall be no more pain, for the former things have passed away.' Ryan had called my house when I was sleeping and asked my mother to write that note for me. I felt such peace at that moment because I was sure that God was telling me Ryan would be okay.

When I found out a short time later that Ryan had passed away I became so angry with God, I felt lied to. Now I understand what God was telling me. I thought that the only way for Ryan to be okay was for him to be cured and with the people who love him here. I realize now that he is cured and with the Someone who loves him most of all. I wasn't lied to, and God did answer my prayer. Ryan *is* okay, he is with God."

Also available from PublishAmerica

BEHIND THE SHADOWS
by Susan C. Finelli

Born into squalor, Raymond Nasco's quest for wealth and power shrouds two generations with deceit, murder, rape and illicit love. Setting his sights above and beyond the family's two-room apartment in a New York City lower eastside tenement, Raymond befriends Guy Straga, the son of a wealthy business tycoon, and they develop a lifelong friendship and bond. Caught in Raymond's powerful grip, his wife, Adele, commits the ultimate sin; and his son, Spencer, betrays himself and the woman he loves and finally becomes his father's son. Years later Kay Straga stumbles upon the secret that has been lurking in the shadows of the Straga and Nasco families for two generations, a secret that tempts her with forbidden love, a secret that once uncovered will keep her in its clutches from which there is no escape.

Paperback, 292 pages
6" x 9"
ISBN 1-4241-8974-8

About the author:

Susan C. Finelli has lived in New York all of her life and has been a Manhattanite for over thirty years. She, her husband John, and Riley Rian, their beloved cavalier King Charles spaniel, currently reside in Manhattan, and together they enjoy exploring the sights, sounds and vibrancy of the Big Apple.

Available to all bookstores nationwide.
www.publishamerica.com